The land of Peldain was completely enclosed by forest, the only approaches it did not block being sheer unclimbable cliffs and the northern ice floes which no ship had ever negotiated. Men had gone into the forest before, but not for a long time and scarcely any had come out alive. For that reason only a few of the forest plants were known by name: mangrab trees, stranglevine, trip-root, fallpits, cage tigers—all vegetable but more deadly than any beast. Because of that forest Peldain had been regarded, throughout recorded history as totally uninhabitable. Nothing like it existed anywhere else in the world.

But now word had come that there was one unconquered kingdom left—in Peldain's heart. And there was nothing for it but to attack through the forest—the implacable, man-eating forest.

Barrington J. Bayley
in DAW editions:

THE ZEN GUN
THE PILLARS OF ETERNITY
THE FALL OF CHRONOPOLIS
THE GRAND WHEEL
STAR WINDS
THE GARMENTS OF CAEAN
COLLISION COURSE

THE
FOREST OF PELDAIN

BARRINGTON J. BAYLEY

DAW Books, Inc.
Donald A. Wollheim, Publisher
1633 Broadway, New York, N.Y. 10019

PUBLISHED BY
THE NEW AMERICAN LIBRARY
OF CANADA LIMITED

Cover art by Ken W. Kelly.

DAW Collectors' Book No. 640

DEDICATION

For Joan

First Printing, August 1985

2   3   4   5   6   7   8   9

PRINTED IN CANADA
COVER PRINTED IN U.S.A.

Chapter One

"We come to the moment of truth, my lord," an acid voice said at Vorduthe's elbow.

Lord Vorduthe leaned against the ship's balustrade, staring across half a mile of water to the shore. The Forest of Peldain grew right down to the edge of the tideless sea, sending green tendrils trailing out into the sparkling blue. The scene was a deceptively quiet and pleasant one. But beyond the first rank of curiously curved and sinuous trunks Vorduthe fancied he detected a flurry among peculiar verdant growths whose structures were hard to make out at this distance.

He shuddered, and turned his gaze to the other nineteen ships riding with sails reefed, their decks crammed with engines, tackle and armored men waiting for his signal. All eyes were on the forest, either with trepidation, with chafing enthusiasm, or in the case of the sailors, with the anxious hope that the landing could be effected quickly and the ships stood off out of harm's way, or else returned to Arelia.

But as yet Lord Vorduthe gave no signal. His finely chiseled face remained calm as he spoke to the man standing beside him, the only man, it seemed, who was not sweating inside his armor of iron and treated wicker.

"You are sure this is the spot?"

Askon Octrago nodded. Metal squealed as he lifted his arm to indicate the shoreline. "Our Captain has navigated well. There is the bluff and there the reefs. Directly ahead of us the slope of the beach is suitable for us to effect an entry."

A few feet away the Captain himself, wearing a green frock-jacket and peaked hat, was regarding them. "Shall I give the word, my lord?" he asked.

If he did not make a move soon, his men would begin to think Lord Vorduthe was afraid. But he did not reply immediately. He looked again toward the forest.

The land of Peldain was completely enclosed by that forest, the only approaches it did not block being sheer unclimbable cliffs and the northern ice floes which no ship had ever negotiated. Men had gone into the forest before, but not for a long time and scarcely any had come out alive. For that reason only a few of the forest plants were known by name: mangrab trees, stranglevine, trip-root, fallpits, cage tigers, all vegetable but more deadly than any beast. Because of that forest Peldain had been regarded, throughout recorded history, as totally uninhabitable.

Nothing like it existed anywhere else in the world.

"Well, my lord?" Octrago pressed. He grinned, the muscles of his jaw tightening against the straps of his helmet.

He is afraid, Vorduthe thought, and the realization caused him a spasm of alarm. He did not trust the man, and still less did he like him. But King Krassos trusted him, and that was enough. It was why they were here.

He signed to the Captain. "Sound the call."

"Yes, my lord."

The captain put a megaphone to his lips. His bellow resounded across the water, was picked up and passed along the line.

"PUT TO SHORE!"

At the command, sails jerked up to catch the stiff breeze at half mast. Oars angled, dipped and strained in concert, guiding the pulleys toward the shore while avoiding the reefs, and in the bow of each vessel a sailor handled a plumbline and called out the depth.

Drums began to thump, their purpose being to build up the nerve of the invading force just as if it were landing in the face of a hostile army. *Yet what are we facing, by the gods?* Vorduthe told himself. *Trees, plants. How could such things be more dangerous than men? What has spawned this place?*

The formation of ships, twenty in line abreast, became ragged as the plumbsmen shouted warnings. They were now close in to the shore and the bottom was sloping up. Sails dropped, oars plied delicately, sailors kept the galleys afloat with poles. The ramps went down, and on to them, first of all, the fire engines were manhandled.

Again the Captain roared through his megaphone. "RELEASE FIRE!" Strings were jerked, matches swung, and from the mouths of the engines on the ramps there swooshed gushes of chemical fire, licking at the jungle, burning, blazing.

Now everything was up to Vorduthe and his men. He leaped on to the ramp, coughing and choking in the acrid fumes. Through the smoke he could see the vegetation curling and writhing and blackening as the exhalation died. Then he was splashing in the shallow water, yelling encouragement to his men who were shouldering equipment down the ramps and on to the ashy beach. Beside him Octrago was panting as he waded sword in hand. And despite the flame, the smoke, the noise and the danger, Lord Vorduthe could not prevent his mind from flashing back to Arelia, and the time when Octrago had first appeared at the court of King Krassos.

Chapter Two

King Krassos of Arelia, Monarch of the Islands, had always struck Lord Vorduthe as a man chafing at the bit, frustrated for lack of conquest.

His father, King Lawass, before him had already united all the islands, bringing them under the Arelian crown and so ending centuries of inter-island warfare. In his youth Krassos had been heard to murmur bitterly that there would be nothing left for him to do, for on the ocean-bedecked world of Thelessa only the sprawl of islands bejeweling the Pan Sea were habitable. The three small continents were either ice or volcanic ash, lava plains and scoria.

Outside the Hundred Islands, as the unified kingdom was ceremonially called, only Peldain was capable of supporting life, and that life was a sport of nature, a forest so deadly that not even Krassos, for all his thirst for adventure, would think of venturing there. Therefore, although Peldain, lying to the south of the northern continent of Kurktor, was somewhat larger than Arelia, his main island, King Krassos found his dreams of achievement thwarted, and excitement to be gained only in the occasional uprising among one or other of the subject populations. Yet, despite his disappointments, he became a firm and respected ruler. He never failed to make himself available on the petition dates due each island in turn, and he meted out fair and just treatment even to the southernmost island of Orwane, whose people were generally disliked because of their peculiar brown color.

Barely a hundred days previously Lord Vorduthe, Commander in General of the seaborne warriors, had been summoned to the king's palace in Arcaiss. There the king had presented to him a man whose general appearance was as strange, though for different reasons, as that of the Orwanians themselves. His eyes were a flinty blue, and his skin uncommonly pale, like limestone. His hair was coarse and a bright yellow in color, resembling straw. His features, too, were odd, with high jutting cheekbones. To Vorduthe, his face was like a statue of the head of one of the leaping deer of Arelia.

"Lord Vorduthe," King Krassos said, "meet Askon Octrago, of Peldain."

The name fell unfamiliarly on Arelian ears, and Vorduthe found the provenance incomprehensible. He nodded distantly, looking at the man and wondering from what isle he hailed.

"Did you not hear what I said?" the King continued casually. "Octrago claims to have come out of the Forest of Peldain."

Vorduthe curled his lip. He took the remark as a joke. "Then he would need to be made of stone, as he appears to be."

"Not even stone can survive in that forest, if what we are told is true," the king added softly.

"Quite so."

Then the stranger spoke, using the Arelian tongue but with a sharp, almost strangled accent. "Just the same, I come from Peldain. I will tell you what I have told His Majesty. You are mistaken about the forest. It is indeed as hostile as you believe, but it does not extend over the whole of Peldain, as you have always assumed. It forms a hedge around my country, between thirty and forty leevers deep. Within is a fertile, fair land inhabited by people like myself."

Vorduthe looked toward his monarch. Krassos was smiling. "The stranger has been interrogated at length," he said. "If he is a liar, he is a convincing one."

"Forty leevers of Peldain forest still sounds impassable to me," Vorduthe replied, looking back at Octrago. "How did you cross it?"

"By means of a special route known to me which avoids the greatest of the forest's severities. Even so we suffered much difficulty. Of fifty who set forth, only five survived to reach the sea, where we put out in a raft whose frame we had carried with us. Had our preparations been less hasty, we would have fared better."

"Then you are not alone? There are others of you?"

"I fear not. For over ninety days we drifted at

sea. We of Peldain have no experience as sailors. When an Arelian ship picked us up, I alone was left, my companions having died of thirst and myself nearly so."

Krassos nodded. "He was in poor shape, that much we do not need his word for. And he comes from none of our islands, if I am any judge. But speak on, Octrago. Tell Lord Vorduthe the reason for so desperate a venture."

The stranger drew himself up. He held his head high. "I, Askon Octrago, am the rightful monarch of Peldain, but I have not been permitted to take my throne. I suffer, my lord, from treason. On the death of my father, the revered King Kerenei, my cousin Kestrew gathered together a gang of ruffians and claimed the throne for himself. Peldain is a peaceful country, my lord. The king commands no armed forces. I was forced to flee for my life. Yet there is nowhere in Peldain where I could be safe. Therefore I and my loyal companions resolved to seek help from the islands we knew existed across the ocean."

King Krassos took up the tale. "And now Octrago offers to become my vassal, in return for help in regaining his kingdom." He clapped his hands. Vorduthe saw that his eyes were sparkling. "That's it in a nutshell. What do you think, Vorduthe?"

Vorduthe pondered these remarkable words. It was not surprising that Krassos was aroused by the tale. The possibilities it opened were, indeed, enticing. . . .

"What, exactly, are you proposing?" he asked

Octrago, tilting his face in the typical Arelian quizzical manner.

"A comparatively small force is needed to take the kingdom itself," Octrago told him smoothly. "Peldain has never known external enemies—the forest itself has been sufficient defense. And it is the forest that will be the greater foe. With my guidance, and proper preparation, enough men could get through the same route I came by. The rest should be easy. Later, I believe this route could be strengthened, the forest driven back. Peldain would have regular intercourse with the Hundred Islands—and would be added, I pledge, to King Krassos' realm. That I rule as his loyal vassal is all I ask."

"This matter needs thought . . ." Vorduthe cut off his own words. He could see that, in fact, King Krassos had already made up his mind. Here at last was a chance to do what his father had done, and moreover, to nearly double the size of the kingdom. The temptation was too strong to resist.

But now, from the shadows at the side of the audience chamber, another figure stepped forth. It was Mendayo Korbar, a member of the Defense Council and a squadron leader under Vorduthe's command. He wore a kilt made of pieces of beaten silver, sword-shaped and riveted to a belt. On his feet, sandals of bark leather. His torso, gleaming with oil, was bare save for the straps that held his weapons.

With hostility, he gazed on Askon Octrago. "Sire, how can you trust this man?" he said bitterly to

King Krassos. "He says he is a king. Yet all we know of him is that he was picked up out of the sea. He speaks the same language that we speak, when even among the islands different tongues may be heard, yet he claims to come from a land with which we have never had contact! I say he is an impostor, and that there is no country of Peldain. The forest covers all of the island."

Octrago, stepping toward Korbar, moved in and out of the bars of sunlight that shone from the high mullions of the room and made a grill pattern on the tiled floor. When the light struck his head, his straw-colored hair seemed to flame.

His voice, with its weird accent, became cold. "The son of a royal household does not permit one of inferior rank to call him a liar," he said. "Though I am a castaway in a foreign land, I am ready to meet and deal with that slight."

He too wore an Arelian kilt, though of strips of stiffened reed paper dyed in a rainbow of colors, and in addition a tunic of light green flax. The king permitted him to carry weapons, and he bore a sword, carrying it in the Arelian fashion, hilt downward, the blade slung up and passing under the left arm to jut up behind the shoulder, held in its scabbard by a clasp. Clicking open this clasp, he drew the sword. "Take back those words."

"Indeed I will not," growled Korbar. His own blade whistled free and he waited for Octrago's attack.

It came almost immediately. Korbar was carried back by the first rush and almost stumbled.

Octrago's sword edge nicked his forearm and spattered drops of blood. He quickly recovered, and for a short while the two blades flashed blindingly in a brilliant display. It was clear that Octrago, though fighting in a style different from that taught in Arelia, was Korbar's equal.

King Krassos and Lord Vorduthe watched fascinated at first, but then the king became alarmed at the thought of losing either man. He shouted with displeasure and leaped down from the dais where he had been seated.

"Enough! Put up your swords, I say!"

The clash and sparkle ceased. Octrago's sword slithered up its sheath and the clasp clicked as he turned to bow to the king. Sullenly, Korbar did the same.

"I have heard tales spun as convincingly in the market place, sire," he grumbled. "I repeat, he is a storyteller, a tool of insurrectionists who wish to draw our forces away from the Hundred Islands!"

"If you are right, you will have a chance for revenge," Krassos promised him. "I am tired of you both: leave me. Not you, Vorduthe. I would speak with you."

After Octrago and Korbar had departed in different directions, Krassos beckoned Lord Vorduthe close. "So what is your opinion?"

"For one who is supposed to come from a land without war, he is handy with a sword," Vorduthe said doubtfully.

"He was not trained in Arelia, I'll warrant."

"Unless he is a master of subterfuge," Vorduthe admitted. "Still, I think there is some merit in what Korbar says. There is unrest across the water. There may be a need to forestall rebellion shortly. I do not think it safe to split up our forces at present."

"Ah, that is why I cannot come with you," Krassos said sadly. "I must remain here to deal with what may arise. I will tell you of my decision. I believe this man Octrago tells the truth. He has described this land whence he comes, its geography, people and customs. Its beasts, and the predacious trees of the forest. Did he invent all this? I do not think so."

"It is odd that of fifty who set out, only their leader survived," Vorduthe remarked.

"Hm. Well, it is the leader who is strongest. And doubtless his followers were prepared to sacrifice themselves for their rightful king. You had better learn to get along with Octrago, Vorduthe, for you and he are to be comrades-in-arms. My mind is made up. I wish you to organize an expedition as quickly as possible. Octrago will brief you. Together, devise means of getting our forces through the forest. When you have sketched out a plan, come and talk to me about it."

"You know, sire," Vorduthe said in a low voice, "that I have reasons for not wanting to be away on a long campaign."

"Yes, I know, Vorduthe," Krassos said with a hint of compassion, "but you are the man to lead this expedition. I want no other. Besides, your absence may not necessarily be a long one. Once Peldain is conquered I will appoint a garrison commander, and you can return home to your wife."

"Thank you, sire."

"Then I expect to see you in a day or two."

Vorduthe bowed to King Krassos as the monarch turned casually away, flipping his cloak of
woven purple grass over his shoulder, and saunter-
ing through an arched exit from the audience room.

The king's palace was a graceful structure of
gleaming white limestone, decorated with large,
brightly colored clam-squirt shells, and with thin
sheets of a smooth iridescent material resembling
mother-of-pearl, a costly material taken from the
internal lining of trench-mouths, sluggish beasts
inhabiting the shallows surrounding the Hundred
Islands. On leaving, Lord Vorduthe first made his
way along the docks of Arcaiss, where ships were
forever arriving and departing, so that the dazzling blue ocean looked like a board game on
which rested slowly moving pieces in carved and
painted wood. Despite the exhilarating sea breeze,
the warmth and freshness of the day, and the
stirring noise and color of the wharves, he knew
he was greeting the prospect of adventure in a
strange land with the wrong feelings. In his heart,
he agreed with Mendayo Korbar.

To one side of the bay, the land rose steeply.
Slowly, Vorduthe mounted the sweep of steps
that brought him to his house, overlooking both
the harbor and the shore barracks of the seaborne
warriors he commanded. He pushed through the
gate-screen of long, cool palm leaves, crossed the
scented garden, and entered the airy interior of
the flat-roofed dwelling.

"Is the Lady Vorduthe awake?" he asked of the servant girl who appeared to receive him.

Briefly the girl bent her head. "Yes, master. She is listening to music."

He could hear the strains of a ketyr coming from his wife's room at the end of the corridor. He removed his sword-harness from his shoulder and placed it in its niche in the wall, before padding down the passage.

Quietly, he opened the door and entered. The ketyr player was bent over his instrument, plucking and caressing the strings with rapt concentration on his no longer young face. The simple waist-cinched robe he wore was crisply white and obviously donned anew no more than an hour or two ago. Musicians visited the Lady Kirekenawe Vorduthe nearly every day. It was one pleasure still left to her.

Kirekanawe moved her face toward her husband in dreamy greeting, but did not take her attention from the music. On the other side of her bed one of the two female companions who nursed and tended her day and night sat silent and unmoving. Vorduthe moved to a cane seat, and waited.

The ketyr sang, skirled, meditated plangently. At length the player paused for long moments, as if he had finished; then he broke into a furiously fast and rhythmic dance theme, which slowed first to a lilt, and then to a languorous plodding sound. Finally, with two evenly spaced, deliberate-sounding notes, he ended.

Kirekanawe sighed, closing her eyes, and then

opened them to look directly at Vorduthe. "You are home early."

"Yes," he said gravely. "I have something to tell you."

Kirekanawe but glanced at her nurse, then at the musician. They rose, bowed, and left.

Vorduthe picked up the cane chair and moved closer to his wife's bed. The form showing through the white sheet was that of a young and beautiful woman, but in respect it was deceptive. Young and beautiful it certainly was, but motionless and inert.

"The king sent for me today," he began when he was seated once more. "I have to go away." Concisely he told her what had taken place: of the arrival of Askon Octrago and his tale of what lay within the Forest of Peldain, and of Krassos' orders.

"If all goes well I shall not be gone long," he told her. "The king has promised to recall me as soon as the conquest is complete."

"You must stay as long as is needful," she said calmly. "A man like you should not spend all his time at home."

"Yes, but . . . I do not like to be away from you."

He avoided her eyes and gazed through the gauze of his wide window, through which the garden was blurrily visible. How often had he looked at her, and seen the thought in her mind: *I should die, and then he would be free. But how can I die? No one will do it for me.*

It was four years now since their happiness

had ended. Once it had been her delight to run, to swim, to make love with vigor and abandon. Now she could not even feed herself, and her own wastes had to be carried away by another.

There had seemed hope when it had first happened. They had gone sea fishing together in an outrigger boat, something they did frequently. He had thought he knew the waters well, but a sandbank must have shifted—a bank that hid a barbsquid, buried beneath the sand and waiting for prey. When the outrigger struck, its tentacles had come lashing forth to seize and sting, spray and wet sand flying everywhere. Vorduthe had fought the squid, hacking its tentacles and forcing it to withdraw, but the spine of a barb, thick and green and hard as wood, was left in Kirekanawe's neck. He had pulled it out with his own hands and sailed as quickly as he could back to Arcaiss, knowing there was a chance the physicians there could wash the poison out of her blood in time. And so they had. Days later her fever ended, and she awoke calm and collected—but paralyzed. He had believed it was but a temporary effect of the poison, until, days later still, the physicians told him the truth. The barb had severed nerves in her spine. She would never be able to move anything below the level of her neck again.

She was made as comfortable as was possible. But no amount of love could erase the frustration he knew she felt, or her sadness at knowing his sadness.

Chapter Three

Vorduthe ignored the heat that struck through the thick bark of his sandals as he waded through the glowing ashes. All the expedition's equipment was coming on to the beach-head amid a cacophony of shouting and a groaning of timber, carried in narrow, broad-wheeled wagons designed to file through the thickness of the forest.

The task completed, the noise lessened. The ramps were withdrawn, dragging through the water. There came a call from the fleet captain: the ships pulled away, sent into reverse by the plying of oars until they lay in deep water where they would wait a day or two and then, if all went well, sail for the Hundred Islands. They would return in half a year's time.

And on this smoking beach were eighteen hundred men, a more than sufficient force, Octrago claimed—even allowing for the quite heavy casualties they would inevitably suffer in passing through the forest—to conquer the interior. In the wagons were supplies, building materials, but,

most of all, fuel for the fire engines, the weapons
on which they mainly depended to get them
through.

Everyone was staring at the charred fringe of
the forest: at the burnt boles, the criss-cross tangle of stems, the singed but still green canopy
that seemed to tremble and reach out. . . .

Octrago was probing at the ash with the sword,
frowning. Suddenly there came a cry from not far
away. A serpent harrier (the formal rank of the
ordinary seaborne warrior) was trying to lift his
foot from the ground. He grimaced with pain.

Darting to him, Octrago slashed downward with
his sword, slicing through ash. Suddenly released,
the serpent harrier hopped away. Some kind of
root was wrapped around his ankle.

"Trip-root," Octrago explained briefly as Vorduthe came close. "I thought there would still be
some about. It would have amputated his foot, in
the space of about a minute."

He looked up at Vorduthe, his straw-colored
hair shining through the metal strips of his helmet. "Are we ready to move, Commander?"

Vorduthe nodded. "Pick the spot."

By his own account, Octrago had passed this
way before. He smiled faintly as he inspected the
edge of the forest, then pointed. "There is a suitable point for entry. Send a firewagon first, as
planned."

On the cindery shore, amid the rubble of tree
stumps, the expedition was forming itself into a
column. Vorduthe had appointed three squadron
commanders to officer his force: Mendayo Korbar,

Kirileo Orthane, and Beass Axthall. Under them, two score of troop leaders were busy putting the men in order. Between the wagons, each hauled and shoved by up to thirty warriors, the troops were to march two abreast—a formation made necessary by the denseness of the forest perimeter. Octrago had declared that a deft use of fire would see them through this outer, particularly hazardous fringe. About half a mile in, the forest would become less close-packed, and the procession could re-form itself into something less vulnerable.

Men at fore and aft shafts trundled a firewagon into forward position, the muzzle of its firespout poking and waving at the forest like an admonishing finger. A serpent harrier squatted over its fuel tank. In one hand he clutched the swivel lever. The other held the string of the matchcord. His face was grim with anticipation.

Ahead of the wagon two testers walked, carrying poles to prod the ground for fallpits. Vorduthe issued the order to proceed, then took his place behind the leading firewagon, Askon Octrago by his side.

The wagon eased itself into the narrow gap between two blackened boles. The shadow of the overreaching branches fell on them.

And then the world he had always known, the world of sapphire sky and dazzling white cloud, of sparkling azure sea and winelike air, was gone. The forest floor knew only a kind of green twilight, enlivened occasionally by sudden flashes of sunlight that darted through the shifting canopy overhead. Underfoot, the ground was moss-like. As for the trees, they were close-packed and Vorduthe could not for the moment discern any unusual features about them.

By his side, Octrago spoke in a murmur. "In the forest is a large variety of trees and plants," he said, repeating what Vorduthe had heard from him in Arelia while they had planned the expedition. "Remember that only about one in twenty is lethal, but that it is impossible to tell which is which. That is what makes the forest so deadly, so treacherous. A harmless cage tiger looks exactly the same as a predatory cage tiger."

Ahead, the wagon twisted and turned to pass between the tree trunks, which were of smooth, straight bark. While speaking Octrago continued to glance to left, to right, and up, sword still in hand as if he expected to be set upon at any moment by invisible assailants.

Suddenly he pointed up ahead with his sword. "Stranglevine! Call a halt."

Vorduthe bellowed. The wagon creaked to a stop, and he called forward men with cutters.

The vine, a straggly net, hung from a line of trees a short distance ahead. It could be no more than inert liana, but as Octrago had said there was no way to tell by looking. The cutters edged forward, extending their long poles on the ends of which were blades that worked scissor-fashion. The blades sliced and cut, dropping lengths of vine to the ground. Finally the way was clear; the procession pressed forward.

Octrago picked up a length of vine, flexed it

and shook it. "No reaction," he said. "It would turn like a snake if it were killer vine."

Vorduthe looked back over the line that was still entering the forest from the clean sunlight outside, twisting and turning as it wended between the tree trunks. He glimpsed the feathered helmet of his squadron commander Mendayor Korbar, who had been so bitterly opposed to trusting Octrago. They were roughly three minutes into the forest and so far its supposedly deadly ferocity had not shown itself. Could it be that the dangers had been exaggerated?

As the thought entered his mind there came a dull *thwack* and something shot out of a thicket: a pointed bamboo-like shaft which speared down from the crown of a tree. It transfixed a warrior through the chest.

What followed was almost obscene. The other end of the shaft was still anchored to the tree that had launched it. Having made its strike, it began to elevate itself, like a phallus becoming erect, lifting the warrior into the air.

The serpent harrier squirmed and clutched at the shaft. Then he gave one last spasm and hung limp and motionless, thirty feet off the ground.

"Cut him down!" someone demanded in an angry growl.

"No!" Octrago warned. "We must keep going—it is dangerous to linger." He turned to Vorduthe. "This was agreed. The dead must be left where they fall."

"Fall is hardly the word," Vorduthe responded glumly. "But I suppose you are right."

He signaled. Reluctantly, the men left their dead comrade. The column resumed its slow march.

Then the surrounding forest seemed to erupt. It was as if an army of spearmen ambushed the procession. From both sides the bamboo lances lunged down, some failing to find a target, but many ripping through armor and flesh.

The thought came to Vorduthe that his men were like fish in water being speared by stalking hunters. "We are in a spear thicket!" he heard Octrago saying. "Use fire!"

There was no need for Vorduthe to give the order. As the ranks of living spears rose, lifting aloft wriggling bodies by the dozen, the firewagons were already being brought into play. Flame gushed to left and right. Fretworks of fire ran along twig and stem, consuming leaves and flowers. Sap exploded, trunks became pillars of flame.

Acrid smoke obscured the scene. When it cleared, the attack was over. The trees, however, still blazed, crackled and popped. Vorduthe looked aghast at the grotesque honor guard made by the upraised spears and their gruesome burdens. He must have lost fifty men.

"We must move quickly," Octrago gasped, coughing in the smoke and heat. "The forest is aroused. We have to reach more open ground."

"You directed us this way," Vorduthe accused. "Could you find no better path?"

Octrago did not answer, but in his heart Vorduthe had not expected him to. He turned away as archers aimed at their comrades still squirming on the bamboo shafts. That was another rule he had been forced to adopt: they could not carry any seriously injured.

The column started up again, but had walked only yards when a scream came from Vorduthe's rear, accompanied by a gurgling noise.

He dashed back along the line. The ground had opened beneath the feet of a serpent harrier, tumbling him into a pit whose tapering sides were lined with rootlike substance. A nauseating, acrid stench floated up from the hole. The serpent harrier, still screaming, was floundering eight foot down in a bath of acid which came nearly to his neck.

As Vorduthe watched, broad green-brown leaves uncurled from the rim of the pit. In seconds they had made a surface not easily distinguishable from the ordinary forest floor, and the dying warrior's shrieks were muffled.

As Vorduthe tested this lid with his sword and found it of the consistency of wood, Octrago pushed his way toward him. "It's a fallpit," he said glumly. "Our fire engines can't deal with those, I'm afraid."

A warrior's face reddened within the ribwork of withe and metal strip that protected it. "But we walked over that spot ourselves!" he protested angrily. "The wagon went over it too!"

"A fallpit's lid is solid most of the time," Octrago said distantly. "It might allow one man, ten men, even a hundred men to step on it before its muscle relaxes. Beneath, the plant consists of a deep hollow root partly filled with digestive acid. Apart from the lid, nothing of it grows above ground."

He gestured. "Come. Move quickly."

Shortly all the expedition was in the forest, and Vorduthe hoped soon to be out of the dense fringe.

But the next ten minutes were terrifying. As Octrago had intimated, the forest seemed to have alerted itself to their presence. Every half minute or so spears came thwacking into the procession three or four at a time. The two serpent harriers placed in the van to probe the ground both disappeared into the same fallpit, which had resisted their rods like solid earth until it was actually stepped upon. Trip root caught many by the ankles, but this was the least of the dangers since a sword could sever it.

From above, there began to rain on the column brambletangles, as Octrago called them—loose clumps of thorny stems which detached themselves from the treetops. If a thorn or a serrated edge touched skin, death followed in seconds from fast-acting poison. The troops, whose bodies were mostly protected against accidental contact, soon learned to ward off the slow-falling masses with the flat of their swords.

Octrago seemed to grow more nervous and advised the almost constant use of the forward firewagon, so that they marched through a sort of charred, smoking tunnel seared into the deadly jungle. While this made it possible to progress in relative safety, Vorduthe wondered how long his stock of fuel would last at this rate. At length, however, the spaces between the trees began to enlarge, the green gloom to lighten to a viridescent twilight that was almost pleasant. The column filled into a large glade, where Vorduthe paused gratefully. At least one of Octrago's promises had been fulfilled, he told himself.

"Will the going now be easier?" he asked him.

Octrago's reply was a wry quirk of his mouth, and to point to a tall line of bush that barred their path and was almost artificial in its regularity. No end to it was visible, either to left or to right.

"Yonder is a terror-hedge. We must burn our way through it."

"We cannot burn our way through the whole of the forest. Might there be a way around?"

A short, explosive laugh escaped Octrago's lips. "Perhaps, if you care to walk a hundred leevers down into the vales. The terror-hedges criss-cross the forest like a maze. The route we are taking encounters only a few of them."

"Then how thick are these hedges?"

"A few yards, usually. But don't think to hack our way through. The terror-hedge is not named for nothing. If interfered with it writhes and surges like a mad thing so that no one could ever evade its touch. Its thorns do not kill. Instead their poison instills uncontrollable fear into a man, so that he loses his mind and destroys himself."

"Very well." Vorduthe stepped forward and spoke to the fire engine operator, who told him his tank was running low. He summoned a fuel wagon and watched while the viscous liquid was transferred through a waxed fiber pipe.

The column was spreading out as it filled the spacious glade. From now on they would be able to move in a more compact mass, less vulnerable to the forest's vegetable attacks.

Vorduthe mused on what he had learned from Octrago of the geography of Peldain. Their route kept to high ground, once they had climbed up from the beachhead. According to Octrago a bird's eye view would show a forest roof that was more or less even, except where it swept down to the sea at the coastal fringe. Beneath it the landscape consisted of hills and valleys, hidden because, for some reason that was not understood, the forest grew everywhere to the same height. In consequence the valleys were like deep dark pits. In them there would be not the smallest chance of survival, even for a force as large and well-equipped as this.

Out of earshot of Octrago, Mendayo Korbar approached Vorduthe. "The Peldainian says two marches will take us to the mountains," he muttered. "I hope he is telling the truth. I have a sense of foreboding."

"This place would fill anyone with fears," Vorduthe agreed. "But his word has been borne out so far."

He turned as a strangled cry interrupted him. One of the trees that dotted the large glade had undergone some kind of convulsion. It was large-boled, monstrously bulbous near the root, and this bulging trunk had somehow opened up, splitting into stretching segments. Already it was contracting again, but caught in the closing cracks was a serpent harrier who was being crushed like an insect.

The branches of the tree trembled ecstatically.
The warrior's comrades ran to attack the bole
with axes and swords. The tree responded in a
flash, opening and closing once more with a motion the eye could scarcely follow. And in it was
now trapped a second man, whose shriek became
a creaking groan as he was squeezed like the first.

Men fell back in dismay as the fissures joined
and hands and legs fell off to drop to the moss.
Only lines of fresh blood showed where the cracks
had been.

Octrago sauntered over. "Now you have seen
what a mangrab tree can do," he said casually.
"With a reach of twelve feet it is difficult to avoid
in some quarters. Here in the clearing, however
. . . it is hard to avoid saying that your men are
being careless."

While Octrago spoke, Vorduthe saw a man near
the edge of the clearing seemingly swallowed up
by the ground, arms flailing but briefly before he
was gone. With everyone's attention on the mangrab tree, the fallpit had taken its victim almost
unnoticed.

"On the other side of the terror-hedge we should
form up for regular progress, as I prescribed,"
Octrago went on. "Form groups of twenty or more,
moving in clots for a common defense. The whole
to advance in a broad column, with the wagons
on the outside, so that attacking plants will be
surrounded and can be dealt with. Keep up the
men's morale. Assure them we shall best the forest in the end."

"These are disciplined warriors and need no

sweet words from you," Korbar replied in a throaty growl.

Octrago turned away, his ironic smile once more coming to his lips.

The fuel wagon was being rolled away. Vorduthe signaled to the operator. A long gout of flame emerged with a roaring noise from the nozzle, followed by three shorter ones. The dense, prickly hedge, almost geometrically precise in its lines, blackened, recoiled, and began to writhe along its visible length in a shockingly unvegetable reaction. Vorduthe wondered if the forest was, in fact, more akin to animality in nature.

For some moments it looked as though the flames would take hold, creeping through the hedges to either side. Then they waned, flickered and died. Octrago had explained that fire was an effective weapon at short range, but on a larger scale the forest was invincible. It could not be burned down; for some reason, flames would not spread in it.

The operator swiveled the firespout and jerked the matchcord again, filling the air with a smell of burning wood that would have been almost pleasant if it had not been so intense. When the smoke cleared, Vorduthe found he could peer through the gap. He saw woodland, much like that on this side except that the trees stood closer together.

"So, then." Octrago seemed almost amused. "Now the journey begins in earnest."

Chapter Four

In a little over an hour and a half the task of transferring the expedition through the terror-hedge was completed. To begin with there had been more attacks by tree-lances, until the firewagons had once again been brought into play, clearing a safe area consisting of charred moss and smoking tree stumps.

Since leaving the shoreline they had been steadily climbing. Octrago had led them to what appeared to be a broad ridge. The overhead canopy was thinner, the air clearer. Vorduthe began to feel more confidence in his foreign guide.

He surveyed his force as the troop leaders organized the new formation, superintended by their squadron commanders. The brash shouting of the beach landing was gone, and had been replaced by a determination that was almost sullen. Orders were given in low tones, and the subdued air of the expedition, the quiet grunts and murmurs as the wagons were jockeyed into position, the clinking of weapons and armor in an oppressive near-silence was ominous.

Vorduthe understood the new mood. The seaborne warriors were accustomed to fighting men like themselves. It affected their morale to take such heavy losses without meeting an enemy they could identify as an enemy. If they had faced the ravages of wild beasts now, they would have remained of good cheer, but against plants and trees. . . .

Octrago, too, was watching the work with a critical eye. "Don't let them spread out too much!" he warned. "Our survival depends on our numbers—we must punch our way through the forest like a fist. Any who become separated won't stand much chance."

Vorduthe nodded. "Especially if they wander off the route, I suppose?" He glanced at the Peldainian. Several times he had pressed him for a map of the special route that was supposed to make passage through the forest possible. But Octrago insisted on keeping it in his head.

Perhaps the secret was simple, Vorduthe thought: keep to the high ground. But if that was all there was to it, why was Octrago so reticent?

He could think of one good reason: Octrago himself wanted to survive. And the Hundred-Islanders would take special care to protect the life of someone whose guidance they believed was indispensable. . . .

The mass of men and wagons began to move, surging around the tree trunks like an incoming tide washing around rocks but giving them a wide berth whenever they could. Vorduthe noticed that Octrago hung back and fiddled nervously with the hilt of his sword. It occurred to him that the Peldainian wanted to be in the middle of the press so as to take advantage of the strategy he himself had outlined. The idea was that a relatively safe area could be created in the interior of the column, able to deal with threats by force of numbers, by fire—by whatever means lay at hand. To this end, the troop leaders on the periphery had orders to keep the formation compact.

Yet Octrago claimed to have come by this route with only fifty men, Vorduthe reminded himself. In that case, a party as large as this ought to be able to overcome the hazards fairly easily.

After a short distance springy moss gave way to tangled herbage standing calf-high. Vorduthe felt something tug at his ankle. He stumbled, then felt an excruciating pain as though his foot were being severed. In one swift motion he unclasped his sword and struck down through coarse grass and leaf. Something wriggled and attempted to pull him off balance.

"Don't fall!" Octrago shouted in warning. "We are in a patch of the damned stuff! Use your sword and stay on your feet!"

Vorduthe pulled his foot free. From it there dangled a length of trip-root, woody and fibrous and harmless-looking now that it was separated from the parent plant. It creaked as he pried it with difficulty from his ankle.

That it was far from harmless could be seen from what was happening all around. A wagon lurched, the men in charge of it stuck to the ground as if they had blundered into quicksand, their faces grimacing with pain and fear. Elsewhere, too, men were stumbling and struggling, slashing at the grass with their weapons. And some fell, the trip-root quickly fastening itself on legs, arms and necks like the stranglevine to which it was closely related.

Octrago himself was caught. With deft strokes of his blade he freed himself, then loped to the stalled wagon, taking long, tiptoeing leaps. He began scything at the grass, rescuing as many as he could of the haulers.

For some it was too late. A warrior leaned against the nearside wagon wheel, one leg lifted to stare at the red-dripping stump where his foot had been.

The Peldainian did not hesitate. His sword-point went straight to the wounded warrior's heart, sliding between the ribs of his armor. Octrago turned away without even waiting to see the body fall.

"On! Forward! You are too slow! Proceed like this—"

Bending slightly, he swished at the grass before him, scything a path. Where trip-root was revealed he chopped through it, cutting the woody musculature.

"You need your wits about you in this forest," he said disapprovingly when he caught up with Vorduthe. "Your men should be more spirited, my lord."

Vorduthe did not answer. They were leaving

the field of trip-root; the ground was reverting to moss with only clumps of coarse grass and strange flowers with crude, blotched colors. He forced himself to turn around and look back to the bodies that lay scattered about, abandoned to be cut to pieces by the inexorable root network and slowly to add their blood, flesh and bone to this ghastly jungle.

He lingered until the last of the troops into which the force was divided had moved onto mossy ground. For the next half hour they traveled without incident. The ground continued to rise; rocky outcrops appeared. The trees, whether straight-trunked or gnarled and twisted into fantastic shapes as many were, became fewer.

But after a while their path began to slope downward, gradually at first, then more steeply. The eerie twilight cast by the overhang grew deeper. Octrago appeared to hesitate several times, casting his gaze here and there before resuming the march with dogged steps.

Vorduthe caught up with him. "Is something wrong?"

"No, we are on course."

"Yet we are descending. Isn't that dangerous?"

"The terrain is uneven," Octrago responded grumpily. "We can hardly climb all the time. You must trust me, my lord."

"So I must," Vorduthe muttered, and fell back to where he could keep watch on his juggernaut of an army as it wended its way down the hillside. The forest was growing thicker, with less space between both the tall trees that supported the overhead canopy and the variegated species, mostly shorter, that displayed such strange shapes and foliage. Vorduthe spotted mangrab trees, lance trees, and the striped trees that Octrago had warned were cage tigers. So far none appeared to be of the active lethal kind, or if they were they were staying dormant.

The wagons were also carefully steered round the clumps of bush, bramble and other plants for which there were no ready names. Then an indistinct tangle loomed up ahead. It was as if the tree trunks rose from a foggy sea of twig and fern which barred the way in all directions.

Octrago halted, staring at the massed vegetation.

"Well?" Vorduthe asked. "Do we turn aside?"

"Not unless you want to go down into the vales, and you know all about that. It's only a thicket. Call the wagons together. We'll push them forward in a solid wall to trample it down, and walk behind."

"Tell me what dangers lie in this thicket," Vorduthe asked. "You had to come through it on your way to the coast, presumably. How did you manage it?"

"We hacked our way through," Octrago said after a pause. "It held no special dangers on that occasion—but now, who knows? The forest is unpredictable."

With that answer Vorduthe had to be content. Following the Peldainian's suggestion, he had about half the wagons formed into a wedge, while his small and already-battered army clustered behind. The remaining wagons he kept in place along the flanks, as before.

The wedge crashed through the thicket with a crackle and a swish. For some time this, plus the creak of wheels, the clink of armor and tramp of feet, were the only noises to be heard. The air thickened and dimmed; overhead seemed to be an aerial jungle which cut off the light, and through which the wagons were carving a rough tunnel.

Occasionally a wagon would jerk and stop, caught in a clump of vegetation or mass of roots, and the whole procession would pause while it was cut free. Vorduthe would have begun to relax, had he not been aware of the nervousness of Octrago, which made him suspect the Peldainian of hiding the truth.

They were deep within the thicket when the forest began its attacks. He heard a cry.

"Stranglevine—beware!"

It was like huge ropy cobweb that dropped from the trees, swung and snaked through the air, suddenly appearing to seize anything it encountered, gripping and squeezing, lifting wriggling men clear off the ground by their necks, a living skein of hangman's nooses.

But at least it was a foe that could be combatted. With swords, with long-handled cutters, the masses of vine were sliced and hacked, writhing and falling in limp strands and tangles to the ground.

Vorduthe, while slashing at the jerking cord himself, tried to count the number of men who

succumbed to the manic creeper before it was
dealt with. How many had he lost now?

And at this rate how many would he have left
when they entered Peldain proper? He looked
surreptitiously at Octrago. It was not easy to read
the Peldainian's naturally pale face. But Vorduthe
fancied he looked worried.

"Tell me," he said when the stranglevine was
left behind, "do our casualties agree with your
calculations so far?"

Octrago uttered what sounded like a grotesque
laugh. "We have scarcely begun. The time to count
our losses is at nightfall."

He moved away as if unwilling to continue the
conversation and, striding between the lines of
warriors who strained at the wagon shafts, leaped
lightly onto a tailboard, peering over the bulk of
the vehicle to look ahead.

After some minutes he looked back, signaling
to Vorduthe, then dropped to the moss and approached him.

It seemed to Vorduthe, perhaps only in his
imagination, that Octrago was terrified. His bony
face was unnaturally tense. And its green pallor
was not only, he suspected, a reflection of the
viridian twilight through which they were traveling.

"The way is barred," Octrago informed him.
"We shall have to break formation and filter
through the trees."

"Why did you not tell me this before we entered the thicket?"

"Remember, we were moving in a smaller group the last time I passed this way."

"So you were ... I wonder how a party as small as yours managed to defend itself against the stranglevine we just came through. Large numbers were decidedly an advantage there.

"Exactly," Octrago said acidly. "You can see for yourself why so few of us made it to the coast." He paused. "Actually, we did not come upon that particular patch of vine. I do not claim to be retracing our path yard for yard. Or, just as likely, the vine has grown since."

By now the wedge was creaking to a halt and Vorduthe was once again obliged to issue orders through his squadron commanders. The wedge broke up. Each wagon, still pushed by its retinue of warriors, began to find its own way through the thicket.

The going was tough. Singly the wagons lacked the wedge's power to trample down the tangle, and more and more often a way had to be cleared for them by hand, stalk and bramble hacked away with swords that now were permanently drawn. Vorduthe noted that Octrago's sword also did not leave his hand, even though he was taking no active part in the work. His suspicion that Octrago was expecting something unpleasant increased. He clicked open the hasp of his scabbard and let his own weapon fall into his grasp.

It was becoming difficult to see what surrounded them, so dense was the thicket. A bole or tree trunk might be only feet away and give no clear indication of its presence or of its species. Vorduthe was not surprised, then, when a voice—it sounded like Lord Axthall's—suddenly shouted out hoarsely. "Beware mangrab!"

At the same time the clumping sound of mangrab trees opening and closing came from several directions, followed by groans of utmost agony.

There was also a crunching, snapping noise. He realized one of the mangrabs had accidentally caught part of a wagon. Suddenly there was an explosion. Through the blurring vegetation, he saw a fireball burning furiously and sending a pall of smoke rising through the branches of the trees.

It was a fire engine the mangrab had seized.

Bellowing to the men to keep going, Vorduthe trudged doggedly on, keeping to the path flattened by the wagon ahead. At length the stench and crackle of the flames were left behind. And now the thicket began to grow somewhat sparser, though the trees remained as close-pressed as before and were hung with liana-like creeper. Luckily it stayed inert, swaying slightly; it was not stranglevine.

Vorduthe stepped from the path and slashed with his sword at the standing stalks. He moved a few feet to the side, placing his feet gingerly though he did not think fallpits grew in a place like this, and peered cautiously. He could partly see the outline of a neighbouring wagon trundling jerkily along, until it was eclipsed by a tree trunk.

His momentary carelessness as to his own safety saved him from certain death. When he looked back it was to see a long shaft, a kind of bamboo pipe thicker than a man, that had lowered itself from the opaque verdure overhead, aslant like the tree-lances they had encountered earlier. Its lower end hovered above the spot where he had stood, hunting to and fro as if searching.

The shaft, no doubt, was hunting him. It had sensed him; it had lunged, and it would have caught him had he not at that moment chanced to step aside.

Where was Octrago? Vorduthe wished to question him as to the nature of this thing. The Peldainian was out of sight, however. Vorduthe skirted the spot, warning off the following warriors who paused to gawp.

The thicket petered out quite suddenly a short distance farther on and the wagon rolled over clean moss. Hereabouts the forest was an eerie, semi-darkened palace whose columns were ragged rows of tree trunks, decorated with gargoyle-like bark of twisted, ravaged boles. The overhead canopy shut out nearly all light.

Peering through the gloom, Octrago heard a rustling sound. Then a swishing and a slithering.

He looked up and saw scores of shafts, like the one he had recently avoided, descend swiftly from the foliage. It was like seeing a second forest interpenetrate the first; or, perhaps, like the massed feeding tubes extended by a certain bottom feeding marine animal: for each shaft seemed to have selected its mark and went to it unerringly.

Sword, bow and lance were no good here. There would be only a brief, wriggling struggle as the muzzle of each hollow tube dropped over the head and shoulders of its victim. Then, a loud *thwack* as the serpent harrier abruptly disappeared.

Forewarned, Vorduthe dodged the shaft that sought him out and threw himself onto the legs of a warrior who was already engulfed to his shoulders. But Vorduthe's strength was quite insufficient to extricate him; he let go only just in time as the harrier vanished up the tube like an insect being sucked up a straw.

Not all who sought to rescue their stricken comrades in the same manner were quick enough to give up. Tumbling to the moss, Vorduthe saw more than one dragged up a shaft still clinging to a pair of legs.

He rolled, sprang to his feet, and ran, to see that the dreadful columns were everywhere: his whole army seemed to have fallen foul of them.

Suddenly he heard a muffled yell from a familiar voice, and whirled to locate its source. Beass Axthall, one of his squadron commanders and a lord in his own right, had been caught by a tube! Vorduthe recognized the insignia, the unique pattern of the armored kilt. But before he could even make a move, Axthall was gone!

The progress of the procession had ceased; the expedition was in total disorder. And now a new menace appeared—but, unlike the shafts, one which had previously been described by Askon Octrago.

They dropped in almost leisurely fashion from the overhead murk: greenish lines, looking like elongated stems from some innocuous flower,

whose ends sported caplike buds or petals. Like
the shafts, they appeared to have some way of
sensing animal presence and they also had the
power of movement, for they twisted and turned
as they descended, until they fell daintily on the
heads of warriors busily fleeing from the lunging
tubes.

One might have thought the helmets the men
wore would have afforded some protection. Not
so: the caplike cups were so pliable they pushed
themselves between the strips of metal and withe
to clamp directly to the skull, fitting as neatly as
the cap of an acorn.

In utter horror, Vorduthe watched men lifted
aloft by the dozen, the stems withdrawing as if
they were fishing lines being reeled in. How the
caps managed to grip a man's skull so tightly was
a mystery. But up in the cover of the branches
Vorduthe could vaguely see his warriors dancing
and writhing, and he could hear them crying in
agony.

He knew that they would hang there like grotesque fruit, all the nutrients of their bodies gradually being drawn out.

A troop leader staggered up and almost collided with Vorduthe. His face was pallid with
fear.

"*Danglecups!*" he gasped. "*Danglecups,* my
lord!"

"Yes. Octrago told us of these."

At least it was possible to fend them off.
Vorduthe's sword scythed the air, severing a green
cord that seemed to have been making for the

troop leader. The danglecup cap flexed itself as it lay on the moss

And not far away there was a blur of motion followed by a sickening thud mixed with the crunch of metal. A warrior had fallen to his death from far overhead. A stalk projected from his helmet, and a danglecup clung to his scalp. The sword with which he had managed to hack himself free was still clenched in his fist.

The troop leader's tone was pleading. "What shall we do, my lord?"

"Fire is our only weapon." Vorduthe pointed with his sword. "You take that wagon. I'll take the other one."

The crew of the fire engine had either been plucked from it or else had joined the other warriors who were huddled beneath it for protection. Sliding his sword up his scabbard, Vorduthe vaulted at a run onto the operator's perch.

No new tube-shafts were descending now. Those that had already appeared seemed sated by their activity, or perhaps they were only capable of applying their suction once. Indolently they were withdrawing. But danglecups there were in plenty, and one was dropping straight at Vorduthe with frightening speed. He swung the nozzle to his highest elevation, pointing it up into the trees. Frantically his feet worked the pedal boards up and down, pumping oil. He snatched up the matchcord and reached out with it as the stream began to issue in a fountain.

The satisfying gout of fire that answered his efforts reached far when aimed upward, assisted by its natural inclination to rise. Its fringe caught the danglecup no more than a dozen arm's lengths from Vorduthe's head and burned it to a crisp.

By now the troop leader had managed to get his firespout into action. From both engines billowing clouds of fire boiled up to the tree cover. Vorduthe turned his muzzle in a wide circle, spreading conflagration among the lower branches.

But suddenly his firestream died, the spout dribbling the last few drops of oil. The wagon had been in the van of the expedition, and it had drained its tank.

Vorduthe jumped to the ground. He reached beneath the wagon and roughly dragged one of the men hiding there into the open. Then he started kicking at the others.

"Cowards! Come out and fight! I'll kill any man who doesn't fight!"

"Fight who, my lord?" groaned a voice. But about a dozen men crawled into the open, climbing to their feet with shamed but grim faces.

Fragments of blazing twig and leaf rained down. The hanging shafts had become columns of fire.

Beyond the vicinity, however, danglecups wrought havoc as before.

"Those sucking tubes aren't doing anything anymore," Vorduthe told the men. "The danglecups you can use your swords on. So go to it—get those fire engines working!"

Though they were reluctant to leave the glade of safety he had created, he led them through the chaos, eyes constantly on the alert for the deadly caps that still were falling from the semi-darkness.

Now that the terror of the tubes was over, others were recovering their wits enough to take Vorduthe's lead. From points all around came the roar of billowing flame. The gloom of the forest turned to lurid incandescence. And slowly, as the danglecups burned and the foliage overhead became a canopy of fretted fire, the expedition began to move again.

How much fire do we need to get us through this hell? Vorduthe asked himself. *How much fuel is left? And what happens when it is gone?* In their panic the warriors were using it wildly, and he gave orders for the spouts to be used only when necessary. Gloom returned, and the attacks of tubes and danglecups became only occasional.

At last Askon Octrago appeared. Vorduthe noticed that the front of his armor was stained green, as though he had been lying on his belly in the moss. He seemed distressed, and at once approached Vorduthe, laying a hand on his shoulder.

"I'm glad you came through, my lord. That was a rough passage."

"You never told us about those shafts that drag men up inside them," Vorduthe accused him. "Why not?"

"Those are shoot-tubes," Octrago told him. "I had hoped we wouldn't meet any of those, that's all."

Vorduthe didn't believe him. He thought the Peldainian had probably kept quiet about them for fear of deterring the expedition from setting forth.

How much else had he withheld?

"What happens to a man who is taken that way?" Vorduthe asked. "He is slowly devoured, I suppose."

Octrago shook his head. "No, it is not like that. Shoot tubes are open at both ends: they work like blowpipes. They hurl a man high in the air, over the treetops to fall down into the vales. If the fall doesn't kill him he faces horrors greater than anything we can meet here."

The appearance of the forest was changing once more. The overhead foliage had thinned, though rarely could one glimpse the sky, and the wagons rolled past new types of tree. Suddenly Octrago stopped, gripping Vorduthe's arm.

"Look. We are in a grove of cage tigers."

Throughout the journey so, Vorduthe had been seeing the striped black-and-white trees Octrago called cage tigers. They had all proved harmless. He was surprised, therefore, at Octrago's sudden alarm.

True, the tigers were numerous here. Of all the plants so far encountered they were the most predatory-looking: bizarrely shaped, as though about to pounce like animals, even though they clearly consisted of timber of some kind. Their foliage was sparse, and they stood barely ten feet in height.

"Too late to think of going round," Octrago rumbled. "Best to get through as quickly as we can. Order a speed-up."

"We should form up in some order," Vorduthe rumbled. "We are all over the place."

"Later," Octrago advised tersely. "Let's get through the grove first."

Vorduthe concurred. Those who could do so hurried ahead. The wagons too increased their pace as much as was possible, the men at the shafts sweating with the effort.

Octrago was stepping carefully, as though afraid his footfall would set off some trap, and was eyeing the striped boles which, now that Vorduthe thought of it, could almost have been carved by the hand of man, so smooth and strange were their misshapen forms.

"You seem afraid," he murmured to Octrago. "Do you advise the use of fire?"

"No. We must conserve the fuel. The tigers cannot take us all. *Aagh*—it begins!"

His exclamation was in a tone of anxiety and resignation mixed. And now Vorduthe realized why he was so concerned.

The cage tigers were virtually impossible to avoid or to defend oneself against. The sight was incredible: the mangrab trees had been able to reach twice the length of a man, but these could pounce much farther—so far that there was no place in the grove where one could be safe. They seemed to leap, to spring, to bound like an animal, but with such suddenness that the eye was bedazzled to know what was really happening. In an instant the cage tiger regained its rooted spot—which it had not in fact left—and the reason for the first part of its name became apparent. The stripes had opened up, arranging themselves into the bars of a cage, roughly square in shape though with rounded corners.

Within the cage there crouched a man.

As if by some group instinct, a score of tigers had struck within seconds of one another. Vorduthe paused to study the scene. So far, those trapped seemed unharmed. They shook the bars or tried to pry them open. Some set to work with their swords.

"Kill them quickly, and let's be on our way," Octrago urged. "This is no place to linger."

"We shall set them free," Vorduthe insisted.

"There is nothing you can do for them. The wood of the cage tiger is harder than iron. It will not even burn. Come."

Octrago loped to the nearest cage tiger that contained a victim. His sword thrust once, skillfully, between the bars of the cage, between struts of armor, into the breast of the caged warrior. The serpent harrier, who had looked on his approach as if expecting assistance, twisted his face in an expression of suprise and pain as the blade entered, gasping as he died.

Bleakly Vorduthe joined the Peldainian, looking into the cage at the slumped body of his follower. "What fate would have awaited him?" he said.

"Death in a fallpit is quick and easy compared with what a cage tiger holds in store. This tree makes a leisurely meal of what it catches. When some hours have passed, the cage starts to contract, until the bars hold the victim tightly without any power of movement. Then the inner surfaces seep digestive juice, very gradually, no more than a smear. First the skin is burned through in strips, then the inner tissues, then through to the inner organs. His suffering would not have ceased until he died of thirst.

"But we have one advantage now. Those caught give us a route through the grove. Pass the word around: a tiger will not strike twice, and other tigers will not come too close to another of their species. Come."

Octrago was off, sprinting to the next victim, whom he dispatched, then looking around for another to give him safety.

Vorduthe looked after him in distaste. But soon, he found himself doing the same.

Chapter Five

"It will be dark soon," said Octrago. "Make camp here. I don't see any dart-thorns and it's as good a place as any."

Since the shock of the attack by the massed shoot tubes, the invading army had fought its way through the forest for another three hours. The men were exhausted, numbed by seeing their comrades being continually picked off, though the assaults lately had come singly rather than in droves.

Vorduthe's mind held a catalogue of ways to die, one or another of which he seemed to have witnessed every few minutes: danglecup, fallpit, mangrab, trip-root, stranglevine, shoot tubes, cage tiger. . . .

Then there were the dart-thorns. There seemed to be several species of these bushlike plants, which shot out their thorns at random whenever anyone passed within range. Sometimes the thorns merely lodged in the skin and caused death by poisoning, quickly and almost painlessly. Some, however, were able to enter the body of their target, leaving only a puncture hole behind. The victim would complain of a stinging sensation as the thorn burrowed inward. Then, minutes later, he exploded, fragments of his innards and raiment flying in all directions.

For some moments afterward the spot would be enveloped in a cloud of steam. Suddenly generated super-hot steam was the means, Octrago had said, whereby the thorn effected its dreadful result.

Wearily Vorduthe nodded, and called a halt. They stood in a large clearing of the type which they had been coming across occasionally since the terrain began to mount once more. A few trees, not very large, with yellowish bark dotted it. After Octrago pronounced them harmless men with axes proceeded to cut them down. They were stripped and dragged to the perimeter as part of the barricade.

Few words were exchanged while the baggage wagons were unloaded. From them came building materials: strong flexible laths, staves, poles, and coils of wicker. With these a framework began to take shape within which the battered army could rest.

Vorduthe helped to supervise the work. The barricade itself was twice the height of a man, and marked out the perimeter. Above it was stretched a net, supported on poles and reinforced with a webwork of slats.

Though the forest seemed quiet at present, Octrago had warned that it was liable to become

more active after sunset, and to produce new
means of assault. When relieved of the daytime
task of soaking up energy-giving light, its vegetable denizens became restless.

As soon as the preparations were complete, he
ordered Lord Korbar to make an assessment of
losses of men and equipment. Then he went among
his men as they settled down to light fires and
prepare food.

He found them somber, sometimes almost sullen, though generally there was a dogged determination to continue. Night was coming quickly
under the forest's rankness. The clearing was now
like a huge tent, lit by the glowing campfires.
Outside, a soughing and swishing could be heard.

Vorduthe made no attempt to cheer his men
with false heartiness. They knew they had taken
a drubbing. Instead, he tersely commended their
courage. The Hundred Islands would long extoll
their exploit, he reminded them. They were already heroes.

For this he received the wry nods one could
expect from toughened seaborne warriors. Only
one was temeritous enough to give him the muttered and obvious reply, "If any of us get back to
tell about it, my lord."

And it was an ordinary serpent harrier, not
even a troop leader, who said to him bluntly: "Do
you trust the Peldainian, my lord?"

"Why do you say that?" Vorduthe retorted
sharply.

"When we came under the shoot tubes he was

down on his belly like a snake, hiding under a wagon."

"And how many weren't under the wagons, if they could get there?" grunted another who was skewering a piece of dried fish to place over the fire. "He knew how to save himself, that was all."

The first man persisted. "I can't see that this forest is any less ferocious than we have always believed. The Peldainian tells us it's a relatively safe route. My lord, will we come through? And if we do, can we get back again?"

Despite that the warrior was voicing his own doubts, Vorduthe glared at him. "I'll hear no more of that talk. The king trusts the Peldainian, and that is enough."

Slowly he walked back to the commander's camp. A blaze had been got going. A stew of sea streamer and decapod tentacle slices was cooking. The smell of the food was incongruous, he thought; cheerful and homely in the midst of the most bizarre peril.

He seated himself next to the silent Askon Octrago on one of the cane stools that had been unloaded. Shortly Lord Orthane joined them. And then Lord Korbar returned. He stood over the seated party, glowering down at Octrago.

"A third of our force gone!" he hissed in a low, accusing tone, so that any underlings near should not hear what he said. "Nearly six hundred men!"

Octrago shrugged. "Say, rather, that we have two thirds left," he said in a tone of weary negligence. "Still more than enough to take Peldain."

"Except that we are only halfway through—and

that by your own account! One more march, you say, but we have only your word for it. The forest may be endless for all I know."

"Once again you disparage my word," Octrago said slowly, his tone becoming firmer. "Previously I was a stranger in your country. But this time you stand upon the soil of Peldain, where I am king. Do you hear, my lord? I am king of this land—monarch and law!"

Korbar turned to Vorduthe. "Is this man even a Peldainian? There is trouble brewing on Orwane, and talk of a secret conspiracy involving the Mandekweans. I have been open in my suspicions from the start: that we have been lured away while a revolt is sprung at home. Better that we turn back now and try to make it to the coast, before the fleet sails away."

Octrago guffawed. "There is bravery indeed! Anyway, your proposal is useless. You are in the middle of the forest. I admit the going has been harder than I had hoped—harder than on the outward journey—but it is still the best route, I assure you. Turn back and you suffer the same losses all over again. Your safest course is to continue."

Outside the confines of the camp a rustling could be heard. The barrier creaked with the pressure of something upon it. Throughout the cleared area conversation ceased while men listened anxiously.

Shortly the murmur of talk began again. Vorduthe recalled that he too had urged the king to caution. The idea that a dual rebellion by the island of Mandekwe and the brown-skinned people of Orwane was even now taking place was most disquieting.

But he did not think Octrago could have anything to do with it. Finally he had agreed with King Krassos that the stranger from the sea was a genuine Peldainian.

That did not mean he trusted him in everything. To all doubts Octrago had smooth answers. But perhaps he did not really intend to remain King Krassos's vassal once his kingdom was regained for him. He had promised that a permanent pathway through the forest could be created for regular intercourse between the interior of Peldain and the Hundred Islands. But bearing in mind the strength of the forest even at its presumed weakest point, how was this to be done?

Vorduthe thought of a roadway driven through the terrifying jungle and protected by a high wall. It seemed hardly feasible ... an underground tunnel might be a more practicable proposition ... but Vorduthe still did not know how so huge a project could be accomplished.

He put the question to Octrago. The putative king of Peldain looked thoughtful.

"I have discussed this matter with King Krassos," he said. "At present the people of Peldain have no means of effecting such a safe route. It is you yourselves who have the key—fire engines. You know how to make the special combustible oil you squirt from the engines. We shall distill it in huge quantities and lay it down in a carpet on the fringe of the forest. Then we shall enclose the burned patch in a brick tunnel and repeat the procedure from its mouth. In this way we shall slowly force our way through the forest."

"It could take a long time."

"Probably about a year. It is not so long. We may even be finished in time to greet the fleet when it returns. King Krassos will be able to sail here and visit his new dominion."

Once again Octrago had shown a flexibility of mind equal to all probings. Even Lord Korbar could think of no retort.

"And what of our losses?" Vorduthe persisted. "They are grievous. The discipline of my men is sorely taxed. How many more can we lose, and still hope to conquer Peldain?"

"We shall have enough," Octrago said after a pause. He smiled. "The King of Peldain tells you so. But for the moment, I shall not insist that you address me as is my due."

With that Octrago rose and strolled through the net-covered camp.

Vorduthe followed him. They walked between small fires and knots of men.

"Do you expect tomorrow to be as bad as today was?" he asked. "Tell me truthfully."

"It is difficult to say. It may be that the earlier passage of my party roused the forest to new depredations. We triggered new growth, as it were. But as we near the mountains it should thin out a little, on the high ground. I am confident."

Vorduthe nodded. A range of mountains, called by Octrago the Clear Peaks, separated the forest from the inhabited part of Peldain. That, at least, was Octrago's story. He had promised to show them a pass through this range, though he had warned there would be something of a climb.

"I am deeply puzzled," Vorduthe said. "I have seen no animals in the forest, except for insects. Yet the trees are predatory. They are meant to trap animals, are they not? It doesn't make sense."

"Yes, that's right, there are no animals," Octrago said, almost wistfully. "There were animals in the forest once, but it has killed them all. It still retains its killing power, of course. The forest never forgets anything."

"How does it live? What does it eat . . . ?"

"It doesn't really need meat. These trees can subsist like any common tree, on soil, air and sunlight. Nineteen out of twenty *are* common trees, as I have said."

"But it doesn't make sense," Vorduthe repeated. "Why should any creature, whether animal or plant, develop an ability it doesn't need? That isn't the way of nature."

"You have hit on a mystery," Octrago agreed.

Vorduthe pondered, brooded. Above and around them, the forest swayed. "And you say there were animals here once . . . it is as though the forest has changed in some way, if that is so. Yet as far as anyone remembers, it has always been the same."

"I speak of a time long before anyone remembers," Octrago murmured. "Long before."

They paused as a serpent harrier at a nearby campfire suddenly dropped his mess-bowl, sprang to his feet and began pacing to and fro in agitation, eyed by his puzzled comrades.

"What ails you, harrier?" Vorduthe asked, stopping the man with a gesture of his hand. A look of suppressed agony crossed the warrior's face. He clutched at his abdomen.

"Just a stomach pain, my lord," he said in a strained voice. "It will pass."

Octrago stirred, looked withdrawn. "Were you struck by any dart-thorns, serpent harrier?" he inquired.

"Why, yes, my lord," the warrior said gruffly. "But that was hours ago, and they did me no harm. They must have fallen off as they struck— see, they left hardly a mark."

He pointed through the strips of body-armor he still wore. On his tanned bare skin were three or four pinpricks. Octrago nodded.

"Well, you were lucky, then." He glanced at Vorduthe, then made as if to stroll on. But in reality he merely stepped behind the harrier while noiselessly releasing the clasp of his sword, letting the blade fall quietly from its scabbard into his hand.

Abruptly the harrier screamed and clawed raggedly at the air. From his torso, from his face, from any place where skin was showing, tendrils sprouted and grew with the rapidity of crawling worms.

Then a sword tip flickered from his chest, withdrawing in the same moment. Octrago had dealt a death blow from behind.

The light of life left the harrier's eyes. Yet,

bizarrely, the dead man failed to fall. He rocked to and fro, as if fastened to the ground. His body and limbs remained stiff, hands still clawed, arms crookedly stretched like tree branches. And meantime the tendrils continued to grow, obscuring his face, blurring the outlines of body and limbs.

Octrago rejoined Vorduthe, wiping his sword on the hem of his short skirt. Those at the nearby campfires had risen, and advanced to view the spectacle, dumbfounded.

Quietly Octrago addressed the gathering. "This man fell foul of the worst kind of all the darthorns," he said. "These thorns appear harmless at first. They leave only small marks and one is generally unaware that they have entered the body and burrowed inward. In fact, the thorns are seeds. After a few hours they germinate and feed on the victim's flesh. You can see for yourselves that they grow with astonishing swiftness."

"He is not dead!" a warrior rasped. "He still stands!"

"He is dead," Octrago assured him. "He does not fall because already he is rooted to the soil, and the plant supports him internally as his body is converted into a bush. Yes, he is dead—but only by the mercy of the sword." He paused, looking from man to man. "Spread the word— any man who has been struck by these thorns and thinks himself safe had best kill himself while he may."

With one last glance at the still-transforming bush-harrier he turned and spoke to Vorduthe.

"Burn this plant, my lord, before it begins to spit darts of its own."

Lord Vorduthe fought his feeling of loathing as he issued the instructions.

The army spent a restless night. The surrounding forest seemed to become manic as darkness wore on. It thrashed, it writhed, and intermittently there were loud creaking sounds, almost like croaking shrieks, as though the trees were attempting to uproot themselves or to march upon the intruders. The netting shook constantly; hasty repairs were called for as ragged holes appeared in it. The perimeter barrier came under constant pressure; more than one wagon was knocked on its side.

At intervals blood-curdling screams signaled that another harrier had discovered himself host to dart-thorn seeds, screams which were abruptly cut short as the hapless victim was rescued from his agony by his comrades. Then the camp would flare with firelight as combustible oil was poured on the growing bush and ignited. The stench of burning half-men made sleep almost impossible.

Toward the end of the night panic gripped the resting men. Beneath them the ground had begun to heave and tremble. Octrago, roused from his slumber, barely muttered an explanation.

"I expect it's the forest's root system," he yawned. "It's detected us and is trying to get to us. Don't worry, it won't keep this up for long."

In several places roots broke the surface and waved in the air like tentacles. But Octrago was proved right. In minutes the unnatural disturbance subsided. The roots had exhausted their energy in unaccustomed motion.

Shortly before dawn a rattling noise came from the upper reaches of the trees, followed by a rushing sound and then a prolonged crashing like that of waves during a violent storm at sea. After the initial fright the encamped warriors realized it was nothing more than a rainstorm blown in from the ocean. But only a few drops fell through the netting; the forest absorbed the entire downpour.

The storm finished abruptly, and the air began to lighten with the approach of dawn. Vorduthe made sure the sun was clear of the horizon (though its globe never actually became visible through the foliage) before preparations for the day's march began. There was a hasty breakfast. Then the protective netting was carefully examined. It was found to be filled with dart-thorns of various sizes, some up to a hand's span in length. These were all gingerly removed before the netting was rolled up and the perimeter barrier dismantled.

Not a man had slept except in snatches. Inspecting his haggard warriors, lords Korbar and Orthane by his side, Vorduthe found it easy to read the fear in their faces. But determination was still there, too—if only a grim determination to live.

"One more day's march, my lord?" questioned a serpent harrier, almost pleadingly.

"We march till we are through," Vorduthe told him bluntly.

Once he had checked the fuel wagons the column set out in good order, adopting the same formation that had been used the previous day once they were through the terror-hedge. Probers and cutters led each group. Behind them, where possible, came a firewagon, while other wagons were placed on the flanks.

The experiences of the day before had led to improvisation. Wagons emptied of supplies— mostly drained fuel wagons—had been broken up and the pieces lashed together to give makeshift cover. As many as could walked beneath these mobile roofs which were held aloft on staves, while others huddled close to the wagons.

The constant presence of the forest was preying on Vorduthe's mind. It was as though some great beast, fastened to the ground by roots, were watching them as they crept through its fur.

He asked Octrago about this feeling. The Peldainian shook his head. "No, the forest is not a single creature. It is the same as any other forest, except that its plants prey upon animals and men."

Korbar was walking with them. "The trees seem to act in concert sometimes," he commented doubtfully. "Such as last night while we camped."

"That is not hard to understand. If one member of a herd of leaping deer takes flight, the others will take flight. If one in a pack of legged snakes spots prey and courses after it, the others will follow. The trees sense when others around them are aroused."

They continued with few words, except when Octrago was obliged to act in his role of guide.

Sometimes he merely seemed to prefer high
ground, as Vorduthe had noticed earlier, except
when he steered the groping army clear of some
grove or thicket he deemed particularly hazardous. But sometimes he would peer through the
forest canopy to try to locate the position of the
sun before choosing a direction. For all his seeming negligence, he clearly had a destination in
mind.

Slowly but steadily the forest began to build up
its savagery. The first few tree-lances hit the im-
provised shields with shocks and thuds and sent
their carriers staggering, grateful for the protection. Then, with increasing frequency, there came
trip-root, stranglevine, shoot tube, fallpit, mangrab, cage tiger, dart-thorn . . . all morning the
column ground its way slowly through the jungle, suffering an enemy it could rarely fight, for
the attacks came singly and to have used the fire
engines constantly would soon have expended
the available fuel. Even Vorduthe began to feel
the weariness and despair of being constantly
surrounded by sudden death. It was as though
there never would be an end to this horrid forest.

And he could not avoid noticing that Octrago's
face, too, became increasingly drawn, though
whenever he became aware of Vorduthe's gaze he
put on an air of confidence.

Then, without preliminary warning, a dreadful
combined assault was let loose. The ground opened
up beneath the trudging army as fallpits by the
hundred revealed their terrible maws. Thick clus-
ters of tree-lances and shoot tubes descended,

knocking aside timber shields from tired arms before withdrawing aloft with a grisly harvest. Almost as swiftly, a swarm of danglecups followed, hauling up its own crop of screaming men who as they rose wriggled like dancing dolls.

At the same time was added the slam and bang of mangrabs, whose boles had been hidden by camouflaging bush.

A cry broke simultaneously from the throats of both Octrago and Vorduthe. *"Scatter! Get away from here!"*

But there was no one who needed prompting. Men were running, fleeing to either side of the broad, vague trail laid down by the column. Some became victim as they ran, plopping into acid-filled fallpit roots or lofted writhing upward by clutching green caps. Vorduthe discovered that Octrago was no longer by his side. He had bolted into the forest.

In moments Vorduthe, too, was seeking cover in unknown dangers, scything his sword over his head to slice danglecups that dropped on uncoiling threads, while all around him men went crashing through the undergrowth in heedless fear.

From many came shrieks as they met fresh terrors. But eventually the forest became comparatively quiet. Vorduthe found himself in a small glade. He poked the moss with the edge of his sword, turning it to try to find the smooth dark-green surface he had learned from experience meant fallpit.

He heard a rustling. A troop leader entered the glade. Like Vorduthe, he grasped his sword in his hand. Vorduthe could see that he was near the limit of his endurance, and perhaps was unhinged by his experience. His sword point wavered unsteadily as he caught sight of Vorduthe, as if seeking out his throat. For a moment Vorduthe feared he was about to attack him in his frustration.

He clenched the hilt of his own weapon in readiness. Then more men entered the clearing. The pent-up expression on the troop-leader's face broke; he sagged, and the point of his blade dropped.

Looking around the glade, concluding that here at least they were safe for the moment, the troopers sank to the ground without even acknowledging their commander. Their spirit, it seemed, had finally been knocked out of them.

Scabbarding his sword, Vorduthe strode to the group. "On your feet," he ordered. "There's work to do."

The men glanced up but at first did not move, until the troop leader, in somewhat sullen voice, joined in.

"You heard what the lord commander said. No lounging!"

He turned to Vorduthe, obviously trying to fight off both weariness and fright. "What is to be done, my lord?"

"We have to regroup and recover our equipment," Vorduthe said. He looked chidingly at the seaborne warriors who were forcing themselves erect. "You won't survive by giving up. Keep your wits about you, and don't let your strength flag."

He ventured to the edge of the glade, peering between the trees which hereabouts were fairly close together. He saw men stumbling about aimlessly, and called to them.

He heard the voice of Lord Korbar, also calling through the jungle. Slowly the survivors began to collect together. At first Vorduthe couldn't believe how few of them there were, and he sent troop leaders forth to seek out more.

After a time a white-faced Askon Octrago appeared. "That was a bad patch," he muttered to Vorduthe. "Sorry I didn't spot it in time."

By now they had approached to within sight of the place where the small army had been so nearly destroyed. The wagons stood abandoned, some turned on their sides or bristling with tree-lances which could not dislodge themselves. Far above, if one dared lift one's eyes to a spectacle so horrid, the trees bore human fruit, transfixed by living spears or hanging limply.

"How can we move our equipment out?" Vorduthe asked Octrago.

"With great care," the other replied with irony. "But it will be less dangerous now. The forest is mindless—it works by reflex. Once a plant has been triggered it usually does not react again for a while. So do not delay further."

It was far from easy. So bad had morale became that the men were afraid to return to the scene of the carnage. But when they saw Vorduthe and Korbar put their backs to the nearest overturned vehicle, the tougher troop leaders stepped forward to help. Serpent harriers followed cautiously,

in twos and threes, until finally the whole army—
what was left of it—was at work.

Shortly they were once again making slow but
steady progress, pushing forward while the forest
continued its mindless and savage war of attrition.

The disaster at the fallpit patch proved to be a
watershed for the expedition, a screen that blotted out the world beyond Peldain, and the day
took on the quality of a nightmare. While Vorduthe
resumed the march wondering how much more
punishment his followers could take, the thought
began to be replaced by an eerie feeling that none
of this was happening; that he had died, perhaps,
or was asleep and dreaming. From the glazed
faces and nervous actions of those around him,
he realized that the same flight from reality was
affecting everybody—except, perhaps, Octrago.

He struggled to take a grip on himself; it would
be a disgrace for the warriors of King Krassos to
succumb to psychological breakdown.

But it was hard to avoid feeling helpless as the
hours wore on and his force was steadily, merci-
lessly depleted by all the horrid means the forest
had at its disposal. Then, sometime after midday,
Octrago gave brief warning of a second major
attack.

They had been hacking through thick bush,
when he was alerted by a curious motion ahead.

"Call a halt," he advised urgently. "Ready the
fire engines."

Vorduthe immediately did so, and studied the
object of Octrago's alarm. In their path lay numerous trees of a type he had not seen before,

dwarfs in comparison with the tall trunks that gave the forest its ever-present canopy. Their olive-colored branches were long and whiplike, and thrashed constantly about as if tossed by a strong wind.

Many of the branches bore on their tips fluffy white spheres, resembling large puffballs. Octrago was shouting to Vorduthe to have the fire engines wheeled forward when, as if by command, the whip-branches drew themselves back and flung several dozen spheres at the advancing army.

They flew swiftly at first, until slowed by the resistance of the air, then sailed, then drifted, over the ragged column.

Petrified with dread, most men cowered or dived under wagons. Only one fire engine operator had the presence of mind to swivel his nozzle, swing his match-cord, and send a swath of fire through the setting spheres.

In that moment, the puffballs burst. It was as if a cloud of gnats came into existence and dispersed, all in the space of seconds.

Again the trees threshed, flinging more puffballs.

"Fire engines forward!" Vorduthe bellowed, galvanized into action. "Burn those trees! Burn them!"

But even as the crews moved to obey, the puffballs showed their deadly purpose. Each seedlike particle expelled by them floated on the air by a parachute of silken threads; now it in turn burst to release a puff of violet spores.

If the colorful little clouds encountered nothing, they sifted harmlessly to the ground. Yet where they settled on human skin, a horrible transformation took place. In less than a minute a patch of discoloration could be seen spreading fast over the helpless victim. This quickly thickened to become a slimy carpet. His flesh had become food for a quick-growing fungus. If touched, fungus and tissue fell away together in rotting gobs, revealing bone that, too, was rapidly disintegrating.

"The mould! The mould!"

The disbelieving moans came from those stricken, who staggered about in horror and despair while their comrades fled from them, refusing to deliver the mercy of their swords lest they should receive contagion from the blades. Vorduthe forced himself to ignore the gruesome sight. Like everyone else, he could do no more than hope to escape infection and to keep his mind on the task in hand. For now, at least, was a peril that could be dealt with after the manner of a military engagement. It was indeed fortunate that the fire engines could frizzle the puffballs in midair, or else the fungus-rot might well have consumed the entire army. As it was, only a dozen or so of the second volley won through the criss-crossing firestreams to airburst their spores, and in seconds the trees themselves were writhing, massed with flame, even while letting loose the last of their delicate artillery.

It was then that the forest sent in its second wave: a hail of lances and a rain of danglecups from the taller trees all around. To these, too, Vorduthe responded with his only effective weapon: fire. He realized he would have to forsake all restraint, all thought of conserving the precious fuel. He created a conflagration. Tree trunks roared with leaping flame. From above, there came a snowstorm of burning leaves.

A fuel wagon was pierced by a tree-lance that had been converted to a spear of flame, and exploded. Yet somehow Vorduthe kept his ravaged force together, leading it between burning stumps that had been a grove of whiplash trees. Behind them the fires flourished but briefly before the forest, in its usual manner, magically damped them down. Behind them, too, lay numerous corpses, including those that had fallen with the fungus-rot. These were almost visibly decomposing. They would add their substance to the soil and furnish fast food for the root system—in its own way, the forest was fiercely logical. Perhaps, Vorduthe thought, they would even be the means of regenerating the whiplash trees he had just burned.

While still on the move he took stock of the supplies. By the gods, there was not much left! Yet, at the same time, he noticed a lifting of spirits among his men. They had won a kind of victory.

And as if to concede that victory the forest became quiet. Vorduthe decided to streamline his resources. He called a brief halt and had the fire engines' fuel casks refilled. This left but one full fuel wagon and two perhaps a quarter full.

He ordered the contents of one pumped into the other. He also sacrificed three partly laden provisions wagons, abandoning what supplies

could not be accommodated elsewhere. The empty
wagons were then hurriedly broken up to provide
makeshift shields.

Thus unburdened, a more compact party made
faster progress, winding between the tall boles.
The forest was becoming spacious again, and again
Octrago led them upward. One hour, then two
hours passed, and blessedly there were no more
than occasional single attacks—a lone lance or
danglecup, a fallpit which opened up and not
always caught its prey. There were no more cage
tigers, no more mangrabs. The warriors of the
Hundred Islands began to experience a feeling of
euphoria, and to hope that the time of dread was
now over.

"The forest's fury seems abated," Vorduthe said
to Octrago. "Are we nearly through?"

But the Peldainian merely grunted in reply.
Eventually they were forced to take a downward
path again, following a gentle and almost meadow-
like slope.

Vorduthe knew that exhaustion played a large
part in the mood of relaxation that was being felt.
It was now late afternoon, and he was tempted to
call a halt and camp for the night, in what seemed
a safe spot. But remembering Octrago's promise,
he was eager to be out of the forest before nightfall.

He allowed a short pause for each man to refill
his water bag. On resuming, the head of the column encountered what looked like nothing else
but an extensive fruit orchard.

The trees, like the whiplash trees, grew in the
shade of the great overhang, whose supporting

trunks sprang from among them. But unlike the whiplash trees they were enchanting to look on, smothered in pink blossoms. The column saun-tered to a halt, more to view the spectacle than anything.

The contrast with everything they had been through so far was startling and refreshing. Was this, then, the end of the nightmare? A smiling serpent harrier walked slowly forward, breathing deeply. "Hey!" he shouted. "It's pretty!"

Vorduthe could smell a powerful sweet per-fume the orchard wafted. Askon Octrago came loping from where he had been loitering at the rear of the column.

"Beware!" he called to Vorduthe in a low tone. "Call that man back!"

Vorduthe felt a prickling in his spine. Already the harrier had reached the nearest tree. He was reaching out to pluck a flower.

And then it happened. The tree shook. It seemed to become a cascade: liquid was pouring down it, squirting out from it. An acrid odor blanketed out the pleasant-smelling scent.

Uttering a high-pitched scream, the serpent har-rier staggered back. The tree had doused him from head to toe in its colorless fluid. He flopped to the ground where he writhed in agony, white vapor drifting from his corroding flesh.

"Drench blossom," Octrago muttered. "So in-nocent-looking. At close quarters the scent can overpower one's judgment like a drug. Then it squirts digestive juice."

Mercifully, the acid did its work quickly. The

screams became a gurgle, and stopped. The body ceased its writhing. Bone was already showing.

Vorduthe sighed. "What is your advice?"

"It looks like a large plantation. Send scouts to right and left. If they find no way round use fire again."

"Send men alone through the forest?" Vorduthe said incredulously. "Will you be one of them?"

Octrago shrugged. "I was thinking of your fuel supply. Very well, burn your way through without delay. It will come to the same, I suppose."

"First tell me one thing. You spoke of two days' march, and we are now near the end of the second day. Are we, then, near the landward fringe of the forest?"

Octrago did not hesitate. He looked Vorduthe directly in the eye. "I think not," he said bleakly. "I think there is some distance to go yet."

"Then you lied to us."

"No. I gave my assessment, that is all. As a military commander, you know yourself that everything is subject to changing circumstances."

"Indeed. I am wondering if in fact you know this route at all."

Octrago gave a wintry smile. "Are you then coming round to Lord Korbar's view? That I am an agent of insurgents in the Hundred Islands? In that case perhaps you can explain how I know so much about the Forest of Peldain."

"Even I know that it contains cage tigers and mangrab trees."

"And drench blossom? Shoot tubes? Dart-thorns? So far I have managed to guide us clear of any slime carpets, which are the most to be feared. They are next to invisible, but prefer the moister pastures. But how would you tell which are the moister beds, beneath the moss? I tell you, without my help you would all have perished long before yesterday's nightfall."

Vorduthe's reply was openly cynical. "So is this the comparatively easy path you promised us?"

"It is."

"My army is all but wiped out."

"It is not wiped out. It still survives as a fighting force, and that is all that is needed. Waste no more time. Use your fire."

Vorduthe could think of no further retort, or see any other course of action. The now-familiar billowing heat of the fire spouts played on the deceptively pretty orchard. Soon the wagons were rolling over ash, then pausing and extending the path of flame.

Beyond reach of the gushes of liquid fire, the whole orchard was discharging its acid in an orgasmic frenzy. The mind-deluding perfume, the acrid vapors, the smell of oil and smoke, all mingled to concoct a nauseating stench.

After burning a path nearly a leever long, they broke through to more open ground. Vorduthe proceeded another leever, then consulted Octrago again.

"Is there any point in continuing farther today? The light is fading, and the men need rest."

Even the Peldainian looked tired. "Probably

not," he said. "This spot will do. Make camp here."

As the barrier went up, and the covering net was fitted, it became pitifully obvious how much Vorduthe's army had shrunk. Few trees needed felling: the camp area was far smaller than the previous night's.

Neither would the coming hours be plagued by the intermittent explosions of men into whose bodies dart-thorns had entered. All such men had been slain, frequently in the face of their frantic protests.

Most of the force, after devouring a hastily prepared meal, fell into an exhausted sleep, oblivious even of the pressings of the forest against the barriers. Vorduthe ordered the guard shifts to be changed every hour; any longer, he feared, and the sentinels might not be able to stay awake.

As before, he sent Lord Korbar to tour the camp and make a count of losses. When he returned with his report he was glowering. He cast an accusing finger at Octrago.

"This man has deceived us, misled us—guided us into our own destruction!" he fumed. "Five hundred men, my lord—that is about what we have now!"

Octrago returned to Vorduthe. "This man's loyalty to King Krassos is touching, my lord," he said, "but I grow tired of his calumnies. You must tell him to forebear."

"He has lied to us!" Korbar insisted. "His tale falls to pieces in the light of what we have suffered! If he truly came to sea by this route, then he must have set out with a body of men and equipment at least as large as ours. Why, then, did he have to come at all? He already had the army he claims he needs!"

Korbar was in a fury. Vorduthe could see that only the iron discipline of an Arelian nobleman was preventing him from falling on Octrago's throat, so convinced was he of his treachery.

"Well, what do you say to that?" Vorduthe asked Octrago.

Octrago rose. Vorduthe was suddenly struck by his regal appearance. It was easy to imagine him wearing the pearled shoulder-plates that were the insignia of the kings of the Hundred Islands.

"Believe what you will," Octrago said supercil-iously. "What difference does it make? I undertook to guide you through the most deadly place in the whole world, and that is what I am doing. Kill me if you think it will improve your situation. None of us can tell if he will live through another day in any case."

He strode from the campfire, spurning the bowl of food that was about to be handed to him. Korbar fell silent. For all his anger, he saw the logic of Octrago's words as well as anyone.

As for Vorduthe, he suddenly realized that he had, to some extent at least, fallen under the spell of this putative king of Peldain. The ground of reality had been cut from under him. Only this peculiar foreigner sustained him, with promises that mostly, it seemed, were lies.

Chapter Six

Next morning Vorduthe assembled a force that, if still haggard, was less bleary-eyed than before. Yet when he came to deliver his exhortation, and demanded the same courage in the day's march that had been shown already, few eyes met his.

There would be mutiny, he suspected, but for the knowledge that there could be no turning back.

He took Octrago and Korbar to one side as the wagons were being lined up, and spoke bluntly. "You have not been honest with us," he said to Octrago. "That is evident to me as well as to Lord Korbar. You claimed the forest was little more than twenty leevers deep at this point, yet by my estimate we have traveled thirty leevers already. Tell me now, without prevarication, how much farther we have to go."

"We may have marched thirty leevers, but not in a straight line," Octrago responded smoothly. "To avoid various dangers I was obliged to divert us hither and thither. In this forest you would not be able to keep track of every change in direction, or know where we were headed. As the seabird flies, we have not progressed more than fifteen leevers."

"Then you still say no more than five leevers separates us from safety?"

"Perhaps."

"Nothing but deceit and prevarication!" Lord Korbar burst out, exasperated. "How can you listen to this man, my lord? For all he may know, the forest covers the whole of Peldain, as our forefathers have always believed! I for one have no hope in a kingdom of Peldain—or that he is any kind of king, either."

"That is only your assumption, Korbar."

"Think, my lord. Could a party only fifty strong, without fire engines, have made the journey we have made? It is preposterous. Yet that is what Octrago's story requires."

"I told you only five survived," Octrago murmured, unperturbed as ever.

"*None* could have survived. We have been duped, my lord. It grieves me to imagine what may be taking place in the Hundred Islands."

Vorduthe stared hard at Octrago. "There is something in what you say, Korbar. Yet I do not think our friend is merely an agent of rebels, as you suppose. I will tell you why. If it were the case, he would not merely be leading us to our deaths, he would be sacrificing himself as well. Such self-sacrifice in the service of King Krassos might be believable, but not in the cause of treasonous scum. Askon Octrago, I have noticed, does not particularly want to die. Besides, he does have some knowledge of the forest, even if not as much as he pretends, and how would some rebel in the Islands gain that?"

He continued speaking, but addressed Octrago now. "I do not know what your motive is, but we have no choice except to follow you, King Askon, if such is what you are. But if by today's end we have not emerged from this forest, I shall have you put to death."

The condescending half-smile still did not leave Octrago's lips. "You hold my life in your hands, commander," he said.

The wagons were poised, the army—if five hundred men could be called an army—was formed up. Vorduthe bellowed the order to march.

They traveled several leevers through a region where trip-root was scattered, hidden in knee-high grass. Often, too, stranglevine made its appearance, hanging in masses which would either have to be burned, cut away or simply gone through. Vorduthe could not afford to waste fuel by now and usually it was harmless. But occasionally it would suddenly spring to life, claiming a trooper or two or even those who were attempting to clear it with the long-handled cutters.

Vorduthe became sickened by the regular amputations and stranglings. More and more he was haunted by the image that Lord Korbar had summoned up: namely, that the forest extended over the whole island and they were merely pushing their way deeper and deeper into it.

Either by luck or because Octrago was guiding

them well, they were meeting none of the dreadful mass traps encountered previously, and shoot-tubes, danglecups, fallpits and the rest struck only now and then. Yet, by degrees, nerves were breaking, so much so that toward midday Vorduthe found himself having to spring to the defense of Octrago, the cause of all their troubles.

A fallpit had opened just as a harrier was about to step off its lid. As near as Vorduthe could judge through the coarse grass, he had but a toe-hold on solid ground, while his other foot plunged into the pit.

Only a few paces away, Vorduthe instantly leaped to help the toppling warrior, but he was too late. Caught off-balance, the harrier flailed, howled, tried to rescue himself, but slid down the slippery tap-root. By the time Vorduthe reached the spot he was bubbling in the underground acid bath. All that could be done was to watch helplessly while the lid closed up again.

He became aware of someone standing by him. It was another harrier who had come running. From the stricken look on his face, from the way he stared at the smooth, nearly invisible cover of the fallpit root, Vorduthe realized that this was a friend—a close friend, perhaps—of the man who had just died . . . or was still dying.

The harrier lifted his eyes. His sword was in his hand as he scanned the area until spotting what he was looking for—Askon Octrago, walking behind a fire engine.

"That's the dung-worm who's to blame!" he growled between gritted teeth. Before Vorduthe could stop him he was darting towards the Peldainian, blade at his side with the point held forward.

It was an attack posture the seaborne warriors were trained to use when attacking on land, particularly when mounting an assault up a beach. In such a position the weapon was carried easily and did not impede the rush of the advance. On reaching the enemy the point was thrust forward and twisted in a disembowelling movement, or the blade slashed left or right, or wielded in whatever manner was called for.

Vorduthe shouted a warning, at which Octrago turned and saw all in a flash. He clicked his own blade from its scabbard. He met the forward rush stock still, then in the last moment stepped smartly to his left, a move which would have forced the harrier to strike from the most awkward angle, with his sword-arm at its weakest.

The harrier did not fall into this trap. He circled, seeking an opening.

Octrago brought his own blade into play. Once again Vorduthe noted his unorthodox swordsmanship as he forced the point of the harrier's weapon down and aside, with a practiced flick. Then he promptly stamped his foot on the flat of the blade, tearing it from the harrier's grasp.

In the next instant he had pierced the disarmed warrior through the heart.

The procession came to a halt and a roar of protest arose as the harrier stretched out his length in the grass. Swords fell from scabbards, and first one or two and then a score of enraged harriers sprang toward Octrago.

They were incensed beyond their discipline; they had been driven too far. Vorduthe ran to place himself between them and Octrago, calling on Korbar and nearby troop leaders to assist him. He collided with one running harrier, knocking him bodily to the ground with his bulk. The man lay gasping like a fish, as if confused and not knowing what to do next.

Korbar, two troop leaders and three harriers had answered his call. They formed a ragged line which fended off the first of the attackers with a brief clash of metal. To his surprise Vorduthe found Octrago by his side, breathing heavily and seemingly eager to dip his reddened blade yet again. None too gently, he pushed him to the rear.

The assailants were not, quite, yet ready to cut down their own commander. Having been stopped in their rush they drew back and hesitated, glaring past Vorduthe at the hated Peldainian.

"Get back to your positions," Vorduthe ordered brusquely. "I shall deal with this business when next we camp. And don't imagine you'll escape punishment."

"Isn't it enough for the forest to kill us?" a harrier cried out agonizedly. "Now we have to put up with this so-called guide killing us, too!"

"King Askon defended himself against an assassin, no more. If any of you have a like intention, you must first deal with me."

"He slew an unarmed man!"

"Enough! We continue the march."

"All we are doing is lining up to be killed!" another shouted. "This forest has no end."

Octrago pressed himself forward once more, his head raised haughtily. Vorduthe could not help but admire his courage. Any of the archers standing within range could have felled him in a moment.

"The forest *does* have an end," he proclaimed in his dry voice. "Neither are we far from it. I give you this promise: we shall leave the thickness of this forest before nightfall, provided we tolerate no more undue delays. Keep your minds on the prize to come, and do not falter."

He turned his face partly to Vorduthe, as if to address both him and the troops. "Surely you do not think I aim to lead you to destruction? I need you on the other side of this forest as a fighting force if I am to achieve my aim. Everything is as I have stated . . . our losses have been higher than I hoped, I admit, but that cannot be helped."

With slow, mesmerizing deliberateness, Octrago bent to tear up a handful of grass, using it to wipe the blood from his blade, which he then sheathed. With a further glance at Vorduthe, he turned and retired.

Sullenly, with more grumbling, the column got moving. Vorduthe spoke to Octrago as they walked.

"I could not express my attitude openly. I had to support you. But privately I agree with my men. You had disarmed the harrier—you did not have to kill him as well."

"So you think I should have spared him, so he

might kill me next time it enters his head? That is not my style of doing things."

"He had been driven beyond endurance."

"Then he was eliminated by the rigors of the journey. Don't blame me."

Vorduthe found it hard to be content with such a reply, but it was all the reply he got.

For a further quarter-day the march continued with losses, which though still frequent, were decreasing in severity. They were entering, Vorduthe hoped, the forest's inner fringe. He fancied that the trees were more sparsely grouped, and the covering dense umbrella of trees not so high. It was some time since he had seen a cage tiger, even a harmless one. Occasionally Octrago cautioned the use of fire, which was applied judiciously—Vorduthe did not want to find himself without any fuel at all, with possible dangers still ahead.

The calf-high grass gradually disappeared; they trod soft moss. It was while they were negotiating a level stretch of ground bordered with bush on either side, and dotted with awkwardly placed boles which forced the column to break up and wind between them, that Vorduthe became aware of a hindrance taking place somewhere in the rear.

"*Heave! Heave!* Put some muscle into it!"

The voice was that of a troop leader whose men were trying to rock loose a provisions wagon that had sunk nearly to its axles. Like Vorduthe, Octrago turned to see what was happening. When he located the cause of the disturbance, his jaw dropped.

Suddenly Vorduthe noticed that the moss under his sandals seemed to be loosening, becoming like the flat sea-weed that formed a surface on certain bays and which one could almost walk upon. More wagons were becoming stalled. He saw men treading gingerly.

Octrago screamed.

After what seemed like a timeless age, Vorduthe realized that what he was screaming were words— harsh, urgent, desperate words that tore through his consciousness.

"Slime carpet! Run! Run! No, not that way— through the bushes! For the sake of the gods, get out of here! Forget the wagons—leave them!"

The screamed words hung like tangible things in the air, usurping any authority Vorduthe might have exerted. He had not expected ever to see Octrago panic, yet he seemed close to panic now. Everywhere the moss was breaking up in tatters, like a skin of mold on a stirred jelly. And jelly was how best to describe what was revealed beneath—a light green goo through which men found themselves wading, and in which all the wagons were now sinking gently, as if into a bog.

As the jelly touched the skin of his ankles Vorduthe felt a stinging sensation, and quickly guessed that the stuff was capable of digesting flesh, like so much else in this accursed forest. But now he saw that the slime carpet was not merely a passive devourer. It was becoming active. It was aroused. It developed whirls which sucked men down into it. It extruded tongues which crept up men's legs, seized and held them, inexorably dragging them into its embrace.

It rippled like a pond in a breeze. Then, at the far end, it reared up in a wave like the waves that traveled over the sea in a strong wind, nearly as tall as a man. This wave swept down the whole area defined by the ragged lines of bushes, surging round the tree trunks and standing wagons. It knocked men down like stalks, and where it had passed they lay stuck in the slime like insects in honey, struggling feebly and vainly to free themselves.

Octrago was running through the gelid muck with a peculiar prancing gait. Vorduthe was about to try the same when a tentacle of surprisingly firm, fast-thickening slime wrapped itself round his left knee.

At that moment Octrago turned back. He saw Vorduthe about to be pulled off-balance. He pranced back to him, seized him by the arm and yanked, pulling him free of the slippery tongue.

Already Vorduthe's knee was numb; his left leg would not support him properly. Cursing, Octrago half-dragged him toward the bushes. Though he seemed unaware of it, he was gabbling manically.

"What a fool I was! Missed the signs! Damned carelessness—quick! *Quick!*"

They were not the first to escape the slime carpet and crash into the bushes. All about them were the grunts of men and the breaking of stems. Then they broke suddenly into a tiny clearing, where Octrago looked about him wildly.

"Dart-thorns!" he yelled. "This way, my lord!"

Abruptly the air was thick with the zipping thorns, shot from shrubs and bushes screened by the more innocent varieties they had burst through. Flinging his arm in front of his face—a useless gesture, Vorduthe thought—Octrago pulled him through an opening to clear ground beyond. But it was too late. Vorduthe had been struck by perhaps a dozen penetrating points. Vaguely he became aware that the Peldainian was frantically brushing the thorns from his skin. His senses swimming, he felt a presentiment of death. Then consciousness slipped from him.

Chapter Seven

In his dream Lord Vorduthe found himself drifting, a breeze-driven ghost, through the limpid greenness of the forest. Cage tigers and mangrab trees snapped about him, shoot tubes lunged toward him. But none of them could touch him. He was dead, and insubstantial like sea mist.

So dead that he rose smokelike through the forest's roof, temporarily losing himself in a close tangle of leaf, branch, bud and every kind of surprising growth, before gaining the clear air to go drifting over the dazzling ocean. And suddenly he was in the Hundred Islands.

That was when death turned into a nightmare. Happenings at home were just as Lord Korbar had warned and he had secretly feared. An army of cruel primitives rampaged through Arcaiss, a horde of brown-skinned Orwanians, always the least civilized of the peoples of the Hundred Islands, ever half-eager to revert to the savage practices of their forebears. For the Orwanians had been ardent cannibals until restrained by Arelian conquest, and they still worshipped their traditional god Krax, who ate the flesh of men.

Flame and smoke billowed over sundrenched Arcaiss. In the royal palace the dreaming Vorduthe beheld a terrible sight: the Monarch of the Hundred Islands, King Krassos himself, spreadeagled over a brazier, face contorted, his skin crackling. And in the streets were fires and cooking grids, and the buildings echoed to the dreadful cries of men, women and children who were being roasted alive for the pleasure of the brown savages.

Vorduthe looked up to the headland where his own home was situated. Against his will his spirit was drawn there, passing through the cool rooms to the interior courtyard. He saw a band of grinning savages, their teeth filed, carrying the paralyzed form of his wife to the fire they had prepared.

One primitive could not wait to see her flesh cooked. Taking a knife of black flint from the waistband of twisted grass that was all he wore, he cut off her nose and stuffed it into his mouth.

Vorduthe's ghost fled, recoiling into the sky among the wheeling wide-winged seabirds, calling out in agonized protest to Irkwele, the great sky god who had thrown down clods of earth into Thelessa's perfect oceans so that man might have islands on which to live. But Irkwele did not reply. Instead a gigantic figure rose cumbersomely out of the ocean. Vast seaweeds draped it. Water streamed down the angles of its face. Sea beasts the size of ships tumbled from its hair.

It was Ukulkele, ruler-god of the ocean who had opposed Irkwele in the beginning. Vorduthe recognized him easily: his image, made of wood and coral and dyed with the inks of various marine creatures, faced Irkwele's across the sacred grove that lay in the exact center of Arelia. Towering over the island, over Vorduthe, the god glared angrily down at him. The ironlike mouth opened; Ukulkele began to speak, in a voice like the sound of the summer typhoons that beset equatorial regions. He had never forgiven Irkwele, he said, for spoiling his unbroken world ocean. He would create great waves to throw against all these scraps of land, washing them away as if they were mounds of silt.

The roaring voices receded; the face of Ukulkele blurred, framed by the blue sky. When it solidified once more it had altered, was smaller, staring down at him with enigmatic sternness.

"He's coming round, my lord," a voice said.

He knew that face. It was troop leader Ankar, a member of Lord Korbar's group. "Where are your troops?" Vorduthe croaked. "Where are they, troop leader?"

"All gone, my lord. Shoot tubes took the last two." The words brought Vorduthe completely to his senses. He was alive. And, he realized with wonderment, there was still blue sky framing the face that stared down at him.

He raised his head. He lay on soft bracken. From somewhere nearby came the gentle sound of flowing water, suggesting that they were camped by the bank of a river. Lord Korbar came into his range of vision, walking toward him. More men were farther off.

Were they out of the forest at last? The spot was hemmed in by trees which included types he had become familiar with in the past three days, but no dense canopy blotted out the sky. Overhead, green and blue were mixed.

Lord Korbar knelt by his side, his face grave. "I am glad to see you may be recovering, my lord. Are you able to rise? Do you still feel ill?"

"Korbar, I have had a dream," Vorduthe muttered. "A dreadful dream. Pray to the gods that is all it was."

He shook his head to shake off the memory. Best say nothing of it, he thought. Some men believed in dreams.

"What happened?" he demanded. "Why am I still alive?"

"You have the Peldainian to thank, my lord," Korbar replied. "It was he who brushed the thorns from your body before they became embedded; they were of the burrowing type. Their contact introduced poisons to your body, but not enough to prove fatal."

"What is this place? How did I get here?"

"We carried you here on a litter, my lord. You have been unconscious for a good part of the day."

"That was against express orders, Korbar!" Vorduthe was angry. "No injured men are carried!"

"It was at Octrago's insistence, my lord," Korbar said apologetically. "He advised us you would likely recover, and that we needed you. I agreed. There were no dissenting voices."

Vorduthe grunted in displeasure, even shame.

He struggled to a sitting position. "Tell me everything that happened."

The young troop leader dropped his eyes as Korbar told the tale, as if not wanting to be reminded of it. "Most fell either in the slime bed or in the thorn bushes," Korbar said. "A hideous time! The few of us who were left managed to retrieve a few tools and some of the mountaineering equipment we will need, but all the wagons had to be left behind. So, without the protection of fire, we made the remaining journey here, and of the few who remained fewer still have arrived. Luckily we had not too far to go, though only Octrago knew it. We are not actually out of the forest, my lord. This is a sort of sterile spot in it, known to the Peldainian—yes, I grant he is a Peldainian, though none the better for that." Korbar made a wry face. "He tells us the main danger is over. We now take to the water."

"Where is Octrago?"

"Up the river a short way, seeing to the construction of boats."

"And how many men have we left?"

"Counting the Peldainian, fifty-three, my lord." Korbar's tone became one of deep disgust. "Roughly the number he claims to have set out with."

After resting a while longer Lord Vorduthe was recovered sufficiently to get to his feet and examine his surroundings more closely. All that was left of the effects of the poison was a slight aching in his joints.

As Korbar had said, this was an infertile spot

as far as the forest was concerned, though why
this was when water was plentiful nearby he did
not know. Perhaps the soil was unsuitable, he
thought. Many trees had died and consisted of
husks. Others were withered, their foliage yellow.

One type of plant, of somewhat sinister appearance, he had not seen before. This was an expan-
sive tree with soft trailing fronds, almost inviting
one to enter its enclosing shade. But among the
fronds were what looked like huge seed-pods,
gaping wide open, two or three times the size of a
man. From the open lips of the pods fringes of
slim tentacles reached out, no thicker than a finger but extending well beyond the shade of the
trees themselves. Plainly they could sense the
presence of men, for they followed their movements yearningly, waving and rippling like strands
of seaweed in an underwater current.

"Those are coffin trees," Korbar informed him.
"Stay away from them, needless to say, though
they do not seem a particularly effective form of
predator by the general standard of the forest.
You can guess from their name what kind of a
trap those pods are."

Vorduthe nodded. For the moment he refrained
from speaking to the tattered remnant of his army.
No more than a score of men were in sight; the
remainder, he assumed, were up-river with Octrago.

As the afternoon turned to evening Octrago's
party returned, carrying with difficulty three boats
of canoelike shape. Briefly their ironlike color
prevented Vorduthe from realizing that they were,

in fact, larger versions of the green pods grown by the coffin-trees. Each looked capable of carrying fifteen to twenty men.

Thankful to be relieved of their exertions, the warriors laid the boats on the ground. An unaccustomed look of pleasure came over Octrago's face when he spotted Vorduthe on his feet.

He came over immediately. "Congratulations, my lord," he said in his dry voice. "I am glad to see that you have survived your ordeal."

For his part Vorduthe displayed no hint of displeasure. "I owe you my life, apparently, but I am not inclined to thank you for it when so many others have perished," he said. "If anything you have done me a disservice. You have brought shame on me, for I too should have perished "

He paused. "Neither do I understand why you should be so concerned for my welfare."

"It is simple enough, is it not? You are my protector, my lord. Without you, how long will these fine warriors keep themselves from my throat?"

"At the rate they have been disappearing you should very shortly have nothing to fear," Vorduthe rasped.

They were speaking alone; Korbar had departed to inspect the canoes. "What have you to say for yourself now, King Askon?" Vorduthe persisted. "We have no army with which to conquer Peldain. What are your plans?"

"On the face of it, my mission would appear to have failed," Octrago agreed, though with less of the glumness that Vorduthe might have expected.

"As for the future, that is decided for us. We can only go on, into the inhabited region of the island, and see what opportunities for advantage there are. Don't despair—fifty of King Krassos' seaborne warriors is a body of men to reckon with as matters go in Peldain."

Vorduthe was inclined to question that in view of Octrago's proven expertise with a sword, but he let it pass.

Octrago pointed toward the riverbank where the boats lay. "Has Lord Korbar explained our situation? Those are the dead husks of coffin pods—big ones. They make perfectly adequate river craft, if trimmed of a few excess parts. We have but to fashion paddles for steering. The current will carry us most of the way, and when we leave the river the depths of the forest will be behind us. There will only be a scattering of trees and plants to avoid."

"Indeed?" Vorduthe looked doubtful. "And what prevents the forest from picking us off as we float along?"

A light chuckle escaped Octrago's lips. "We shall be safe. You will see."

A thought occured to Vorduthe. "How many men could be transported this way? Are dead pods of that size plentiful?"

Though the smile faded from the Peldainian's face, he kept his composure. "Quite plentiful. Any number could be carried down-river, I dare say."

With that, the conversation ended. Every man was told to make himself a paddle as best he could with whatever materials came to hand, using what tools there were or even the edge of his sword. Although darkness would soon descend Octrago advised they should set out straight away. No one had eaten since early morning; none of the food in the stricken wagons had been recovered and he had warned from the beginning that nothing in the forest was safely edible. It could be days before they found food.

Octrago demonstrated how to twist dry leaves together with reeds from the riverbank to improvise a store of makeshift firebrands. Then, before embarking, Vorduthe addressed some brief words to his remaining troops.

"Our experiences," he said, standing before the haggard-faced men, "have been so terrible that few would believe them. What we have come through has never been endured by any Arelian before. But those of us who stand here *have* come through it, and while we remember our fallen comrades, we can take pride in our achievement. Our thoughts now must be for the future. We are promised that the worst is over, and that from now on there will be only human foes to fight, if any."

He paused, looking over the group of warriors, no more than troop-sized. In the eyes of nearly all he saw the same silent question. *We were supposed to be an invasion force. How do we conquer now, being so few?*

"After such disasters there can be no guarantee that any of us will see home again," he continued. "New adventures await us, in a land none of

our kin has ever seen. Put your trust in Irkwele,
and behave, as you have behaved, like warriors of
King Krassos!"

One by one the four pods were lowered into
the water and held fast while the men clambered
aboard, Vorduthe, Korbar and Octrago taking their
places in the leading pod. Then they were cast off
together and maneuvered to the middle of the
fairly fast-moving, but rather narrow river.

Vorduthe marveled at how well the pods performed as boats, standing upright in the current
by virtue of their heavy spines and proving easy
to control by the ship-wise Arelians. The rim of
the pod in which he sat had been cut back to
make the structure more open. Some interior ex-
crescences had also been cut away, leaving the
inner surface dotted with knots and lumps, some
of them serviceable as seats. There were also signs
of what could have been dead veins and slitlike
lips—the remains, perhaps, of the knot's original
purpose as both mouth and stomach.

Swiftly the current bore the boats on; there was
no need to do much more than hold them steady.
The little flotilla was swept beyond the oasis of
infertility and past overgrown banks, past surrounding jungle that grew ever more lush. To
begin with the men shrank behind the protection
of the pods' sides, afraid of the towering trees
which soon completely overhung the stream. Occasionally there would be a flurry of branches
nearby, a lunge of lance or wriggle of danglecup,
but the boats moved too fast to make an easy
target for the vegetable predators and Octrago,

sitting upright in the prow of the leading craft, paid them absolutely no heed.

Vorduthe peered into the water, curious to know what fish or other creatures might dwell there. The water was very clear; he saw a bottom of sand and pebble across which strands of light green weed ran. There were no fish; only some lizardlike things with vertical knife-edge tails and long toothed jaws. They were about the size of Vorduthe's forearm.

"Don't put your hand in the water," Octrago said with a smile, noticing his interest. "They'll have the flesh off it in moments."

The Arelian commander settled back in his place. The trees had joined far overhead, blotting out the darkening sky. Then it became evident that the riverside bushes were growing closer together, forming a continuous hedge which reached ever taller. Peering ahead, Vorduthe saw that the river entered what appeared to be a tunnel.

The tunnel was, in fact, formed of the bushes, which finally overreached the stream to form a curved, matted roof. This, probably was the protection Octrago had spoken of. In gray gloom the boats plunged into the winding corridor, whose coolness and silence, apart from the rippling of the water, created a soothingly enclosed feeling. Sometimes one could glimpse shadowy shapes through the thicket and tangle that roofed the waterway, but mostly it grew ever denser. The forest began to seem a distant threat.

For what Vorduthe guessed might be three to five leevers they wound their quiet way. The sun

went down. Of Thelessa's bright starlight little
filtered through the forest's foliage and less still
through the matted vegetation that made up the
natural tube through which the boats rode. Vorduthe was asked for permission to light brands,
but Octrago held up a staying hand. "Not yet," he
said. "We are not completely blind. We shall
need them for later."

Gradually their eyes grew accustomed to the
near-darkness. Vorduthe could see those around
him as vague shapes.

"The current is becoming sluggish, my lord," a
serpent harrier said suddenly.

It was true. The boat had drifted near the left
bank and had slowed down. Soon it veered cross-
wise to the direction of the river and scarcely
moved at all.

Octrago took a firebrand from the pile in the
bottom of the canoe and after several tries it lit
with the flint he carried. He held the slowly crackling flame aloft.

The flickering light revealed the four boats drifting in brackish, barely moving water, close to one
another and swinging this way and that. The river
had broadened, overflowing its banks. The covering tangle pressed low, barely above their heads.
A short distance farther on it merged into the
water, blocking the way.

"The bushes have choked the stream," Octrago
announced. "We shall have to clear it. Stay in the
boats for the time being—there might be water
lizards about."

At his bidding they paddled the canoes up

against the damming tangle and began hacking with swords and axes. Vorduthe tried not to think about how far the blockage might extend, but shortly it became clear that the bed of the stream was logged with flotsam and completely silted up. They were able to step out of the boats and continue the work while standing on the spongy matting.

At first they thought to cut a path through the bush and drag the canoes over the detritus, to what they hoped was clear water beyond. In the event it proved easier to dig out a narrow channel through which to half-float, half-haul the boats, crawling meanwhile beneath the thorny mass overhead. They labored in darkness, relieved intermittently by the light of a firebrand; until at last there was a sudden rush of water as the final bar of silt was shucked away and the channel made contact with the continuing riverbed.

The water level here, fed only by what had seeped through the blockage, was lower than on the other side, but now it began to rise and the current to quicken. Pausing only to splash some of the mud off themselves, the Arelians clambered back into their boats to follow the current once more.

To Vorduthe's surprise the prow of his boat suddenly dipped sharply. He heard the scrape of Octrago's flint. Sputtering flames gave sight of new surroundings.

The vegetation was gone. They floated now through a tunnel whose walls were of bare rock. The stream had probably entered a hillside,

Vorduthe thought. But at the same time the boats were quickening their pace; they were on a downward slope, descending deep underground.

The river swirled and boiled as it swept through the winding cave. In places the roof was so low that the boats barely scraped through and the passengers were obliged to press themselves below the rough-carved rims of the timberlike pods.

They made their way by the poor light of the briefly burning brands. If the torches happened to die together there was total darkness for a while and the boats bumped against the rough walls of the tunnel and even into one another, but generally it was not too difficult to hold them steady. Soon the stream leveled somewhat. The path which the river had over the ages carved out of solid rock became less irregular, so that Octrago deemed that brands should be lit only now and then. For a lengthy period they proceeded in this fashion, learning by feel how to keep the prows turned forward and how to prod themselves free of the walls on either side.

Suddenly the natural channel opened into a large cavern, its limits indistinct in the light of the torches. The river splayed out into a broad body of water which moved silently but fairly fast in the subterranean darkness, like a wide river approaching a weir.

Octrago shouted to turn the boats to the left and paddle close to the near overhang. Presently a kind of shore came in sight: a big stone ledge rising out of the waterline.

"Beach here," Octrago called.

Stepping deftly from the leading pod as it careened on the rock, he stood holding aloft a blazing brand, facing the others as their sandals trod the damp stone. His words echoed dully as he spoke.

"I have called a short halt here to explain that a tricky pass lies ahead," he told them. "At the far end of this cavern the water divides in two. One part, the greater, falls into a deep fissure and after that its course is unknown to any man—perhaps it plunges endlessly into the depths of the world. The other, the one we must take, leads to our goal."

He paused to transfer fire to a fresh brand before continuing, tossing the expired one into the water where it hissed briefly. "The current will do its best to carry us into the fissure so we must paddle with a will to find the exit. It is essential to keep as close as possible to the left-hand wall. If you lose sight of it then you will know you are being swept toward the chasm and from then on nothing can save you.

"Also, do not lag. I will locate the mouth of the exit and guide you to it, but I shall not be able to linger. If you are not in sight of the boat ahead of you then you will be lost."

There was shifting of feet. "How near is the exit to this fissure?" someone asked.

"Very near—that is the difficulty. You must approach the tunnel mouth with all speed and resist the current for all you are worth."

"It might be easier if the boats were roped

together. We could help one another," someone else suggested.

"No, because one endangered boat could drag the others over the edge with it. Each boat crew must rely on its own strength. Is all understood, my lord?" Octrago raised his eyebrows to look sternly at Vorduthe, and then at all the others. "Good. Then we proceed."

The water looked thick and black and it tugged at the pods as they were pushed free of the ledge and probed forward under the close-pressing rock. At first this was no problem as the current was all in one direction toward the far end of the cavern. But after some minutes the lake's surface under the overhang became plagued with eddies and unpredictable cross-currents. Something seemed to be trying to drag the boats away from the edge of the cavern, not toward its center but somewhere to one side.

Again and again the pods were swung round as if attached to underwater ropes and had to be returned to their course by determined concerted paddling. Octrago, using a succession of torches, leaned as far over the prow as he could, peering anxiously into the darkness. From ahead there began to come a steady rippling sound.

"Make ready!" he called at last. "The flow now becomes swift!"

And so it did. Octrago's brand was blown out by the breeze as they were swept forward. Cursing, he spent valuable seconds kindling another with his flint. When the flame strengthened, Vorduthe saw the expanse of water racing away from them to the right, surging aslant, and beyond it a great black hole over whose lip it streamed.

There was a big waterfall in the hills of Arelia. Vorduthe had visited it often. The falling stream plunged with a continuous roaring noise, and it filled the air with spray which sparkled in the sunlight. How different was this! The dark water was sinister in its quiet. There was no roaring: only the subdued rippling. No spray: just the cavern's usual dampness in the air.

Did the stream fall to such a depth that its eventual crashing into whatever lay below could not be heard? Vorduthe suspected that the underground lake was fed by more rivers than the one they had come by, which he did not think could supply such a mass of perpetually falling water. Octrago gave a shout of encouragement: he had spotted the mouth of their escape route. But the current was strong and at its flood.

Such a hurrying onrush would have been impossible to resist had not the water begun to whirlpool, swinging into a curve on its approach to the chasm. The periphery of the vortex never reached the gaping hole, however; instead it split off, drawn through the tunnel mouth opposite. Keeping to this narrow band of water was the only way to avoid being dragged over the edge.

All oars were plied on the right-hand side of the boat in the desperate effort to stay under the overhang. The far end of the cavern loomed up. Vorduthe was unable to make out the tunnel entrance, but Octrago presumably knew where it was for he called to direct the boat a little to the right—a frightening instruction for it seemed to mean turning into the vortex.

Vorduthe looked aft to check the progress of the following two boats. He was dismayed to see only a flickering light some distance off, which while he watched disappeared.

He nudged Octrago. "I can't see the others!" he hissed.

Octrago swung his head round. He frowned, the flickering flames making his face grotesque. "We can't wait for them! If we slow down we're finished!"

He turned his attention back to the rock wall. By now Vorduthe could make out a black shadow there. Then, visible on the surface of the water, the current parted.

"To the left"! Octrago shouted. "Take us to the left!" The men in the body of the pod responded with a final attempt to extract yet more leverage from their paddles. Then the boat suddenly shot forward and was carried into the hole in the wall.

No sooner were they safely inside than Octrago grabbed a paddle and frantically turned the boat athwart the current, trying to jam it in the tunnel. "Light brands—as many as you can!" he urged. "And call to your comrades—shout for all you're worth!"

There was a *thunk* as the stern struck the tunnel wall, then the long pod swung round until it lay close alongside and was held there by hands clinging to any unevenness they could find in the rock. As the torches blazed the symmetrical outlines of the tunnel were picked out in sharp relief. Hoarse bellows echoed up and down it. *"This way, lads! Over here!"*

Answering calls came from over the water. Vorduthe feared that the other boats were hopelessly lost and that he was hearing the last doomed cries of men about to be turned over the lip of the chasm, but soon the shouts came louder and flickery light showed itself at the mouth of the passageway, and first one boat and then the other floated downstream toward them.

He breathed a deep sigh. "Thank the gods!"

Octrago was smiling, clearly pleased with the outcome of the operation. The newcomers checked their progress as they approached, pressing their paddles against the walls.

"Excellent!" he declared. "Well, let's get going. We should be through by morning."

They cast off, allowing the stream to carry them. The tunnel stretched ahead, a straight, continuous bore. Unlike the route from the forest to the cavern, it was clearly the work of man.

On and on the three boats moved, gliding gently through the darkness, for here there were no hazards and therefore little need of light. If a boat bumped into the wall of the canal it was easily pushed off before it jammed itself. Vorduthe arranged for the men to get some sleep, resting in shifts. And he even slept an hour or two himself.

At one point they encountered an obstacle. Light from a brand revealed a rockfall that partially blocked the way. A spell of work was required to clear the obstruction sufficiently to allow the boats to pass. They continued, until Octrago who had spent the whole time peering eagerly into the blackness, announced he could see light. In the minutes that followed the illumination grew, streaming in from the glowing circle ahead.

They had come through.

Chapter Eight

On its final approach to the exit the formerly circular tunnel narrowed, and the roof rose to elongate itself into a pointed arch. Through this constricted passage, framed at the opening with cut stone, the boats floated gently into morning daylight.

The slightly quickened water rippled. The travelers had emerged from what Vorduthe saw was a vertical gash in a moundlike hillside shaggy with grass and shrub. The underground stream issued into a peculiar gorge, or valley, bounded by cliffs that resembled long barrows or promontories projecting from the hill-mound on either side of the fissure.

The cliffs were oddly rounded, bulging, overhanging the valley floor a little, their vaguely undulating outlines twinned. Downstream they parted steadily so that the valley widened, as they tapered to about half their original bulk at their extremity. There, they ended in sudden up-

thrusting crags that jutted like weirdly shaped
sentinel towers.

Beyond the stark buttes, at what distance it was
hard to estimate, a mountain range filled the horizon, its peaks rising steep and jagged against
the early morning sky: the Clear Peaks of which
Octrago had spoken.

As the valley became wider the stream meandered, becoming to all intents and purposes a
natural river which eventually carried the boats
onto a level plain. Astern, the valley with its
diverging barrow walls receded. The Forest of
Peldain had vanished; but the new landscape over
which the river wandered was not without its
vegetation. Dotted about it were trees whose predatory aspect was familiar to anyone who had experienced the terrors of the forest: limber, swaying
trees with long whiplashes which they cast constantly about as if searching for food. Octrago
regarded them with a glum expression. He seemed,
Vorduthe thought, disappointed to find them there.
But nothing was said, until one of the trees loomed
up rooted to the side of the river, its lashes easily
reaching to the opposite bank.

Then he ordered the pods out of the water to be
carried half a leever downstream, giving the whip
tree a wide berth.

The river journey continued. The sun rose higher
in the sky and the Clear Peaks became gradually
larger. By now everyone was hungry, but Vorduthe
refrained from asking Octrago when and how food
might be found. Seaborne warriors were tradi-

tionally scornful of comfort and there were no complaints.

The tallest peaks were streaked on their pinnacles with something white that shone in the sun. When asked about this, Octrago stared at him in bemusement.

"It is snow. Do you not know what snow is?"

"But that is only found in the far north."

"It also forms at high altitudes, where the air is thin. There are no tall mountains, then, in the Hundred Islands?"

Still mystified, Vorduthe shook his head.

"Luckily we shall not have to climb so high," Octrago assured him. "We are less than well equipped to do so, I assure you."

When the mountains came near enough to seem oppressive the river swung to the west, seeking lower ground. Vorduthe queried if it was not time to quit the boats and proceed on foot, but Octrago advised that they should wait awhile.

The reason soon became apparent. A grove of trees came in sight. Not whip trees, or anything resembling the horrors of the forest, but on the other hand they were equally unlike anything the men from the Hundred Islands were used to. Within the lush foliage their branches formed rough grids, somewhat like cooking-grids, and from these hung bulbous fruit.

"This is it," Octrago announced. "We disembark here."

As soon as the prow of the pod hit the bank he stepped from it and carefully scrutinized the grove, as though to make sure it was safe. Then he moved into its shade and reached up to pluck a yellow fruit.

It almost fell into his hand. Without hesitation he bit into it, chewed, then gestured to the others.

"Eat. It's good."

The men moved into the little orchard. The fruit had a thick but soft and edible skin. The pulp within was juicy and tasted delicious.

They quickly ate their fill and most would have been glad to relax for a while in this pleasant spot, but Octrago was eager to be moving. At his urging their scant equipment was taken from the boats, which he then unceremoniously pushed into the water and allowed to drift downstream.

"Gather fruit," he then said. "We shall need provisions."

"And how do we carry it?" Mendayo Korbar asked dubiously. They had no satchels; no way to carry except with their hands.

Octrago had an answer to this. He beckoned to Korbar, and led him deeper into the grove, looking about him in search of something.

They came to a tree of a different type: slender, with sharply raked downpointing branches. From them grew unusually large pale green leaves, broad and fat. Octrago plucked one and showed it to Korbar, then peeled open the edge nearest the stem and inserted his arm.

The leaf was hollow. Opened up, it made a serviceable bag or satchel, large enough and strong enough to hold a dozen or so of the yellow fruit. Octrago then split the stem into a loop by which he hung it over his shoulder.

"Nature provides," he said curtly. "The bag can hold water, too, and if the lips are pressed together they seal themselves again. The men can pick whatever they need."

Korbar returned to give Vorduthe the news. Shortly the party was trudging toward the mountains.

The afternoon saw them climbing the foothills, after which the ground rose steeply and they toiled up the lower slopes. Vegetation grew sparse. They entered a wilderness of boulders, cracked clifflike blocks of rock and patches of scree.

After they had gained considerable height Octrago paused and bid Vorduthe and Korbar look back. The plain lay below them. But now the large hill from which they had emerged by boat lay revealed in its outline—and it held a surprise.

It was a massive sculpture: a long hill carved into the recumbent figure of a naked woman. Trails of wheat-colored grass represented her spread tresses as she lay on her back. Pointed hillocks, thrusting up from the main mound, were her breasts. Her arms were smaller side prominences, lying limp.

Her legs were apart. From the cleft in her crotch the stream issued, to pass between her thighs and go wandering over the landscape.

Everyone present marveled at the sight. Fascinated, Vorduthe tried to imagine how much labor must have been involved in such a task, how much time it must have taken. And what was its purpose?

"It was done a long time ago," Octrago answered when this question was put to him. There seemed to be a note of sadness in his voice. "I do not know why."

"Then this region was once inhabited?"

"Yes, it was once inhabited. Here we are between the Clear Peaks and the forest, whose fringe you can see."

Vorduthe looked again. Octrago was right. Beyond the reclining female the horizon was banded with a darker color—a malevolent dark green.

"It would not have been visible once," Octrago said lightly.

"You mean it is spreading . . .?" An image came to Vorduthe's mind of the helpless woman being engulfed, eaten, as the forest encroached on her body, burying her in horrors.

"It was less extensive in times past. But have no fear. Its growth will be curbed."

Lord Korbar spoke up. "The route we have taken is essentially the one you followed on the outward journey?" he queried.

"Correct," Octrago told him.

"Then you followed the river from this plain, underground and into the forest. You must have found it most difficult to make such a journey against the current."

Korbar had made no attempt to hide the suspicion in his voice. Octrago barely paused before answering. "At intervals the river reverses its direction. Sometimes it flows outward from the groin of the hill-statue, sometimes inward. We followed the inward flow. This is caused," he added casually, "by the chasm in the cavern. At times water wells up from deep underground, and forces a reversal of current."

Blinking, Korbar stared at the river as it meandered over the plain below. "That's a strange business," he grumbled. "Wouldn't it mean the stream had to flow uphill?"

But this time Octrago did not reply. He turned and led the way up a bank of loose shale, pausing at the top and then finding a way through a crevice in the tortured rock.

He seemed a more confident guide than ever he had been in the forest. At length they came to a cliff face impossible to ascend on foot, and here it was necessary to climb. At Octrago's direction the men were roped together in groups of five or six. Octrago led the way; where hand and foot-holds could not be found he made them by means of the tools that had been made for the purpose, chisel-headed picks that opened cracks in the rock where metal struts could be hammered firmly in place.

Once the strut he had left came out under a warrior's foot and the luckless fellow plunged, nearly dragging his companions with him. But the climb was neither long nor difficult, and at the top Octrago found a ragged pathway that wound up the steep mountainside.

In places the trail, while mostly natural, looked as if it had been cut artificially. From now on the ascent became a simple hard slog, punctuated by occasional climbs or sometimes scrambles over

masses of rock which barred the way. The air
grew cold and frequently they were obliged to
pause for rest.

By late evening they had reached a saddleback
ridge between two peaks and were able to look
down on both sides of the mountain range. To
the south was the plain, with its naked reclining
female—smaller and barely visible in the dusk—
and the dark viridescence of the forest.

Vorduthe looked eagerly down the northern
slope, hoping for his first glimpse of inhabited
Peldain. The view was swathed in mist, in which
it was difficult to make out anything. The trail
they had followed continued, becoming a ledge
on initially sheer cliffs. After that, the slope was
gentler and considerably more negotiable than
that they had come by.

Dusk was quickly enveloping everything below. "To continue after dark would be foolishly
dangerous," Octrago said, "even though the exer-
tion would help keep us warm. We'll settle ourselves here. It means a cold night for us, I'm
afraid."

"Well, at least the downward path looks easy
enough," Korbar remarked. "Shall we reach our
journey's end tomorrow? And if we do, what
then?"

"I am afraid we have not yet finished climbing."

Octrago pointed to the nearest westward peak,
a craggy monolith whose shadow was now falling
over them. "We have to make our way farther
along the range before it is safe to descend. The

route is a bit difficult. But don't worry, we don't need to go as high as the snow line."

Korbar stared at him in stupefaction. "This is ridiculous!" he exploded. "The way down is clear before us! Furthermore, this is a route that has clearly been used before!"

"That is only how it appears," Octrago said, mildly but firmly. "The route I have chosen is in fact the easier."

A long pause followed. "That requires explanation," Vorduthe said edgily.

"Very well," Octrago replied, in an equable tone. "The truth is that we have not left the forest behind us yet. It surges round the east limb of this mountain range and though you cannot see it, it lies directly below. The path you think so simple and easy leads directly into a deep forest vale—one of the deepest. You know what that means."

"Then we can descend, and make our way along the mountain range at a lower level but still above the tree line," Korbar insisted.

Octrago shook his head. "Not possible."

Korbar tensed. Around them, the men were opening their leaf-packs, gulping water and biting into the refreshing fruit, and sharing their rations with those who had lost theirs during the climb. Korbar was breaking an unspoken rule by arguing in front of them like this, but Vorduthe could see he was repressing an inner rage.

At last his feelings broke through. "I know that you have lied to us, misled us, pretended to know what you do not know. Why do you wish to direct us away from what is obviously the better path? Perhaps it is simply that you have not yet killed enough of us. Perhaps you want to arrange for what few of us remain to fall to our deaths— just what is it you do want, King Askon Octrago?"

"A kingdom," Octrago replied simply.

Korbar turned on his heel. He walked to the edge of the northern escarpment and stood there, staring into the gathering darkness.

He turned his head as Vorduthe joined him, and spoke low but quickly. "In my view we have only one real choice, my lord. We should put Octrago to death and proceed as we ourselves think fit. He will only lead us to fresh disasters."

"You are still convinced he doesn't know what he is doing?"

"I am."

"Then what reason could he have for taking us by the harder route? It makes no sense."

"Perhaps he needs no reason. Perhaps he is a madman. In any case he is lying to us. I feel it."

"Clearly he has some knowledge of the region, while we have none," Vorduthe said placatingly. "In our ignorance, we are forced to trust him— though I grant suspicion comes naturally."

Korbar merely grunted. Vorduthe walked back to the main group. His warriors had been eyeing the exchange with interest.

"Which way do we go, my lord?" asked one with a grin.

"We go the way our guide directs," answered Vorduthe, and gestured to the mountain.

No one questioned his word. The men were

relaxed, knowing that nothing they faced now could be as bad as what they had already survived.

As the night wore on it grew cold. This was an unaccustomed experience. To the men of the Hundred Islands the world was always a warm, balmy place, even at nighttime. They had no coverings for themselves, and nothing with which to make fire, and they wore only their traditional scant raiment. Chilled by the thin air and the biting breeze, they huddled in the lee of a granite outcrop, and first shivered and then cursed with pain as the cold did its work.

At long last the sky lightened and the stars diminished in number. The sun rose glowing from the horizon, slowly dispelling the last of the stars as it spread its ceiling of dazzling azure.

But as yet it did not cast much heat. The warriors jigged about and clapped their arms to their sides, trying to force some warmth into their frozen bodies.

After a brief breakfast they set forth, Octrago leading the way. This time there was no ancient trail. They walked, then clambered toward the peak, aiming for its north face. Eventually the slope became precipitous; roped together, they crept step by step along it, each depending on the others.

Once, the warrior on the end of the line lost his footing, and as he fell the rope slipped from around his waist where he had tied it insecurely with numbed fingers. They both watched and heard him tumble and plunge, roaring with rage. Then,

when he was gone from sight and his cries were
no longer heard, they continued without comment.

Another problem was the onset of a wind that
threatened to blow them off the mountain. A distant observer would have seen them clinging to
the mountainside like flies, scarcely moving at
all.

By mind-afternoon they had passed around the
bulk of the mountain and were on another saddleback, more broken and at a higher altitude
than the one they had set out from. Here they
rested, and ate and drank the last of their rations,
while Octrago scouted ahead to pick out a route,
taking Vorduthe with him.

It was evident he had no knowledge of this part
of the range, only some idea of the ultimate destination. They returned having chosen a way up a
ramplike incline choked with boulders. It ended
in a natural hollow, and here they elected to
camp for their second night in the mountains.
They were even higher now and the air was thinner and colder, but at least they were sheltered
from the winds and breezes that sucked every
atom of warmth from flesh and bone, and despite
hunger, thirst and agonizing cold, they were fa-
tigued enough to be able to sleep in snatches.
Next morning it took some time to coax life into
their stiffened and complaining limbs. Vorduthe
insisted that a lengthy spell be spent on physical
exercises before, on empty stomachs, they resumed
the journey, for now came the most difficult climb
of all. From here on it was not possible to tra-
verse the side of the mountain, which presented

a precipitous north face, almost a sheer cliff as if
it had been sliced off by some giant's axe. Instead
they were obliged to toil up crags and scars, always searching for some route by which they
might clumsily find their way. The wind whistled
about them and once a shower of finely pow-
dered snow blew down on them—a unique experience, for few had ever seen or touched snow
before. Eventually, after what seemed an age of
slow effort, they came over the mountain's shoulder and descended on the other side until Octrago
called a halt on a convenient shelf.

He looked around, scanning the nearer peaks
as though satisfying himself as to his whereabouts.
Requesting that the two commanders follow him,
he then walked to a granite outcropping, crouched
down behind its cover and motioned to them to
do the same. He peered over the rough granite,
keeping his head low.

"Don't show any more of yourselves than you
have to," he murmured. "Well, there it is. Now
you have a human enemy to deal with. It should
make a pleasant change."

He was gazing at an outjutting crag farther down
the mountain. So haphazard was its outline that
it was some moments before the Arelians recognized it as an artificial structure.

It was a mountain stronghold, a moderately
sized castle of rough stone that had been cut,
probably, from the granite of the mountain itself.
Studying it, Vorduthe realized that from his present vantage point it was vulnerable. The rampart
faced north, to ward off attack from below. In the

rear it simply merged with the mountainside; one had but to clamber down and step on it.

The builders had clearly not reckoned on attack from this quarter. Octrago was speaking, and soon explained why this was so. "The fortress is excellently placed. It is perched atop a precipice and commands the path along the foot of this mountain range. Approached from the north, it is impregnable, and neither may anyone pass below it against the wishes of its guardians. Since there is only one pass over the Clear Peaks, and to reach it one must take that road, there is normally no way the fastness can be attacked from the rear. As military men, you will quickly appreciate the advantage that now lies in our hands, especially if we achieve surprise."

"So that is why you made us suffer in these heights," Vorduthe commented grimly.

"You will not regret it."

"Then I was right!" Korbar burst out, raising his voice despite himself. "The other route *was* the right one!"

"No, you were not right," Octrago responded icily. "You opposed me purely out of enmity. You had no knowledge whatsoever of which was the correct route to follow."

"But you did lie to us. If it had not been for this plan of yours which you kept secret from us, we could have taken the easy path, which I presume would lead us below the fortress."

"As to that I cannot say. The forest does extend round the Clear Peaks, as I told you. Whether it yet cuts off the pathway is unknown. No one has gone that way for a long time. How the guardians in the fortress would react is also uncertain. Were we spotted traveling *toward* the pass we would be stopped by means of rocks and poison fumes poured over the precipice. To be seen proceeding out of the Clear Peaks would no doubt occasion some concern, and puzzlement."

"Why do you constantly deceive us?" Vorduthe accused. "Why did you not simply tell us why you wished to come this way?"

The putative Peldainian monarch shifted position on the cold rock before answering. "Have I deceived you? I tell you as much as it is good for you to know. Perhaps I should apologize for not being more open—I can only say that I act only as a king of Peldain is accustomed to behave. You are expecting me to alter the royal customs to which I was raised."

He paused momentarily before continuing. "But to say I have deceived you is to put too much on it. Matters have turned out broadly as I promised. We are in Peldain, an accomplishment men of your nation previously thought impossible."

A sour look crossed Korbar's face. He seemed too disgusted to point out that the forest had destroyed a small army. Vorduthe shook his head and could almost have smiled. It was impossible to pin down this enigmatic man.

Just the same, he wondered if he would have been as patient had he not been constantly conscious of Octrago's supposed royal blood.

"Well, you had better supply reasons now," he

said. "Who holds this fort, and why should we attack it on your behalf?"

"Because it is the key to Peldain." Octrago's voice became dreamy. "In that fortress is a much loved man without whom no king of Peldain can hope to rule for long, without whom the land itself may perish. My enemies hold him there. Our first task is to free him."

"And just who is this man?"

"He is the High Priest of the Lake."

"Then this is to do with religion?"

"If you like."

"Tell us of this religion," Korbar demanded suspiciously. "What is this 'lake'?"

"It is a lake in the center of the habitable re-gion. It is known as the Eye of Peldain." Octrago smiled mysteriously. "For now, just take it that if we have the High Priest, Peldain becomes con-trollable. If not. . . ." He shrugged.

"We too worship gods, but they do not decide who is king," Vorduthe ventured. "What gods do you worship, that are of such account?"

"Our god is mighty and must be placated at all cost. Well, are you with me? If you need further incentive, let me add that there is but one way down the rest of the mountain and that is through the stairwell whose head is within the fortress and which passes down the inside of the cliff."

A familiar note of sly humor entered Octrago's voice as he made this last remark and Vorduthe knew he did not intend it to be taken seriously. Yet for all the Peldainian monarch's elusive way of speaking, he felt that matters were at last beginning to be made clear.

"Yes, we are with you," he said. "How many men are within the fortress, and how are they armed?"

"Probably somewhere between fifty and a hundred," Octrago said. "Most of the weaponry is aimed at crushing forces below the fort and so need not concern us. Personal arms worn by the soldiery will be broadly similar to your own: lances, bows and above all swords. Of course, we have no lance-men left, and Peldainian swordsmanship differs from your own."

"Ours can prove itself," Korbar growled.

"I don't doubt it."

"The men are tired, very tired," Vorduthe said. "And they will be fighting on empty stomachs."

"We shall rest, and attack after dark. As for food and drink, we have to fight for it."

"And when we have taken the stronghold, what then?" Korbar demanded.

"We proceed into the heartland of Peldain, to claim our own."

Lord Korbar turned to Vorduthe. "My lord, have you considered what our own position may be? I remind you of our purpose in coming here—to gain this land for the crown of King Krassos. Is this still to be done? We shall be pitifully small in number. Why should King Askon here honor his vow? The men of Peldain are not totally without fighting skills, that is evident. Perhaps we shall become King Askon's prisoners—or slain at the earliest opportunity."

Octrago, unperturbed by Korbar's impudence, answered for Vorduthe. "A possibility, from your point of view. But I ask you to remember that you will have Mistirea, High Priest of the Lake, in your possession. You do not as yet realize what an asset that is."

Vorduthe grunted. "Having let King Askon lead us this far, it would be foolish not to trust him now. He is a sworn vassal of King Krassos and knows, I am sure, how we would view treachery. Now let us rest—until nightfall. . . ."

With sore and weary limbs, they edged away from the cover of the rock, to give the news to the curiously watching, waiting men.

Chapter Nine

The pale light from Thelessa's sky of massed stars
threw the craggy stronghold in sharp relief. The
men from the Hundred Islands crept down the
slope, the hunger that gnawed at their bellies
sharpening the tension they felt, while they hoped
that with the mountain at their backs they would
be no more noticeable than shadows.

Vorduthe had spoken to each man personally,
asking him his name. As he answered each man
had smiled with pride—pride at having come so
far, at being able to grapple with the enemy at
last. The fortress jutted out ahead; now Vorduthe
could see where the slope fell steeply away to
become a virtual precipice.

The starlight picked out silvery traceries in the
roughly cut stone. Deftly Vorduthe stepped onto
a walkway that was, in fact, no more than a path
cut between the mountainside and a blockhouse.
Octrago accompanied him; about half the force
followed close behind. Korber, leading the remainder, had descended on the far side.

Sandals falling noiselessly on stone, they sidled to a lumpish corner and edged around. The ground fell away here and the walkway projected out into the air, protected by a parapet. Peering over, Vorduthe saw an abyss, with starlight falling on an indistinct landscape.

Octrago nudged him, and they passed on. In the wall to the left was a broad timber door. Octrago lifted a latch and gently pushed it open.

Within was darkness. A faint murmur of voices came from somewhere below. Octrago moved past Vorduthe; he could be heard moving about, then there was the click of another latch as he found a second door, and a chink of faint light appeared. Vorduthe's eyes made out the shape of the room they were in: it was a storeroom, containing stacks of barrels.

Octrago closed the inner door again and returned, ushering Vorduthe outside.

"First we deal with the sentinels," he whispered.

The walkway widened as they approached the square fortress's forward corner. Letting his head slide slowly around it, Vorduthe met an unexpected scene.

In the front of the stronghold, the walkway became a spacious terrace, on which defensive engines made of timber and metal were mounted. The frontage of the blockhouse was peculiar: it was shaped like a funnel, in which was caught a mass of boulders. The arrangement suggested that they could either be avalanched directly down the precipice or hurled some distance by the engines.

Similar catapults had sometimes been used in the Hundred Islands.

In addition, a series of pipes ran across the courtyard and projected through the parapet. Their beginnings were in squat vatlike vessels fitted with lids. Octrago had spoken of the fortress being able to deploy poisonous vapors. The pipes, Vorduthe thought, were probably the means.

He counted those men on watch he could see. There were no more than half a dozen of them, spaced out along the parapet, and their eyes were fixed on the night terrain below. Constantly to survey the pass at the foot of the mountain was, of course, the most essential duty in the life of the stronghold.

The Peldainians wore thick clothing to protect them against the cold. They carried swords in what was known in the Hundred Islands as the barbaric fashion—slung from belts around the waist, the sword-points trailing, as had once been the habit in some of the more primitive islands. Vorduthe smiled. An Arelian warrior could not help but feel superior to any swordsman who wore his weapon that way.

He looked to the far end of the terrace, and was rewarded by a slight movement. Korbar was there. He signaled to him, then beckoned to those behind him.

Pale ghosts, a dozen seaborne warriors spread across the terrace, picking their targets. The first Peldainians to die did so silently, scarcely knowing it. The next gave a muffled yell. Alerted, the remainder turned, looked startled, gasped, drew their swords—Vorduthe was surprised to see it took them little longer than if they had worn shoulder-scabbards—and made shift to defend themselves.

One did not even get his blade free before he was cut down. The others got barely any better chance to show their worth. In seconds no watchman was left alive.

Vorduthe moved to the parapet. These were the first Peldainians he had seen apart from Octrago, and one after the other he studied the dead faces intently. The racial resemblance was clear for the most part: skin white as limestone, high cheekbones. He pulled back a cowl and saw pale hair which in sunlight might well have been as yellow as Octrago's own.

Grinning in triumph, a trooper pawed at the jerkin of the man he had just killed. "I could do with some of this warm clothing!" he announced. "Hm. It's not cloth. Some animal's skin, I'll be bound."

Vorduthe touched the material worn by the man he was examining and rubbed it between his fingers. It had a velvety feel, but somehow it was unlike either cloth or any animal pelt he knew of. It was hard to say what it was.

The Peldainian's unblooded sword lay nearby. Picking it up, he ran his eye along its edge. The workmanship was fair, but not impressive by Arelian standards.

The hilt, though . . . it fitted his hand snugly, but had a grained feel, like tree bark. He inspected it, and could have sworn its surface *was* tree bark, had it not been so perfectly formed. . . .

Laying it down, he cuffed the trooper who was now in the act of pulling the jerkin from his victim. "Later. You can't loot and fight at the same time."

Lord Korbar reported seeing a timber door on his side of the stronghold too. "Good," Vorduthe said. "Most likely it also gives access to the interior. Take your contingent and attack from that quarter, Korbar—if you find no way through then return to aid us. King Askon, perhaps you would be good enough to accompany Lord Korbar." If they should fail to meet up within the fortress he would worry less about the stolid Korbar with Octrago along to advise him.

Stealthily Vorduthe led his own party through the timber door, then groped his way to the inner door and opened it a chink. Through the crack he saw only what appeared to be a stone-walled passage lit by a guttering bracket torch. But voices and subdued laughter floated up from somewhere.

For a few moments he waited, to allow Korbar and his group to get into position should the room opposite have a different layout. Behind him the warriors were stumbling, cursing and jostling in the darkness; he opened the door a trifle wider to give them light.

At his elbow was one of the four surviving troop leaders, a man named Wirro Kana-Kem. "Be ready, Kana-Kem," Vorduthe whispered. "We go through now."

The troop leader hissed instructions to those

behind him. Vorduthe pushed the door open and stepped through.

To his left the stone passage proceeded to what he guessed was the rear of the blockhouse, where it turned through a right angle. To the right, one wall ended a few paces along and the corridor became a gallery.

Striding cautiously to the start of this gallery, Vorduthe saw what it overlooked: a large common room. At a broad but curiously gnarled table, laden with platters of food and jugs of drink, some fifty men were seated, eating and talking. They all wore garments of the same design: hip-length white surplices on the chests of which were stitched an emblem he could not make out from this distance, and sleek green knee-britches. Piled against the farther wall of the common-room, nearest the front of the fortress, were weapons, helmets, and other fighting garb.

The air was stale and smelled strongly of the smoky torches used for lighting. Vorduthe tried to estimate what the chances might be of cutting off the weapons stack before the Peldainians could get to it—it would save a lot of bloodshed and he could not afford to lose many men. Only one stairway connected the gallery with the floor and that was at the nearer end. Men might run the gallery's length and lower themselves or even leap to the floor, but it was a fair drop.

Then Korbar appeared on the parallel gallery that overlooked the other side of the hall, and almost at the same instant someone down below glanced up and spotted the intruders. The Peldainian looked incredulous, then gave a shout of alarm.

Vorduthe grabbed Troop Leader Kana-Kem and thrust him forward. "Four men to the far end, down onto the floor and stop them getting those weapons—*quick!*"

Kana-Kem in turn grabbed behind him, snapping orders. As he and the men he had detailed raced along the gallery Vorduthe flourished to Korbar and rushed with a howl down the stairs.

From both sides the Arelians poured into the common-room, drawing shrieks of fright and hoarse, confused cries from the diners. But the Peldainians were not long in recovering their wits. They leaped to their feet and fled the table, making for their arms.

Kana-Kem and his warriors had only just reached the far end of the gallery. A serpent harrier leaped, aiming to land on the tabletop. A Peldainian had already snatched up a lance, however. It caught the unfortunate Arelian in midair, its barbed point transfixing him in the chest. For a moment he swayed on the end of the lance, screaming. Then it and he dropped together, and he died.

Undeterred, Kana-Kem and the others came hurtling down from the gallery. Vorduthe vaulted onto the table, loped its length, then jumped down to swathe his way through the press of Peldainians, on whom the entire force of seaborne warriors was now falling.

But the Peldainians fought—by the gods, how they fought! Even when armed with nothing but eating knives they fought, and Vorduthe saw one of his men go down gurgling with such a blade in his throat, thrown from a fair distance.

He reached the far wall to find Kana-Kem by his side. For the first time he was having to deal with Peldainian swordsmanship, and it was disconcerting—but so, he imagined, was his to them. Two and three at a time they came at him, but in a sudden flash of insight he saw how to deal with their characteristic parries, lunges and twists.

One he took through the heart, another fell clutching his midriff. All was bloody confusion. Only a few of the Peldainians had managed to reach their weapons. For others the slaughter was terrible—the Arelians were in blood-lust now, after seeing their comrades slain, and waded savagely, even gleefully, through their new foe.

The unarmed Peldainians still alive panicked, tried to run for the stairways, were blocked by the guards stationed there, and then cowered quailing under the galleries. Suddenly Vorduthe realized it was over. He bellowed an order to stop.

About half the Peldainians had been struck down, for only two Arelians lost. The smell of blood was in the air, mingling with the oily smell of the torch-smoke. The prisoners were herded together and searched swiftly for hidden weapons. There was a movement on the floor. A young Peldainian, chest smeared with blood, raised himself on one elbow. He stared at Askon Octrago, whom he seemed to recognize, and pointed at him with shaking fingers.

"Octrago! You have spilled the blood of the Lake! A curse on you, Octrago!"

At this a thin, bitter smile came to Octrago's lips. He turned away, as his accuser slumped and was still.

Now Vorduthe found a moment to look closely at the emblem all the Peldainians wore on their surplices. It was a stylized representation of a green tree overhanging what appeared to be a pool. Or lake?

"Yes, they are all acolytes of the cult," Octrago said, noticing his interest. "All the garrison are."

Vorduthe frowned at him. "Am I to believe that the High Priest is a prisoner of his own followers?"

"No time for discussion," Octrago replied. "We are not in possession of the stronghold yet—we may still have half the garrison to deal with, and we had best move quickly."

He stepped to the huddle of prisoners. "Where is Mistirea, your master?" he demanded of them.

There was no answer. They only glared at him.

Octrago pointed a jabbing finger and picked out an acolyte at random. He gestured to Kana-Kem. "Troop Leader, kill that man."

Sword in hand, Kana-Kem looked dubiously to Vorduthe for guidance. Vorduthe shook his head grimly and strode forward.

"We are warriors, not murderers," he said.

Octrago flushed slightly—the first time Vorduthe had ever seen him do so.

Then he shrugged and nodded to a door set in the rear of the common-room between the two stairways. "No doubt that is the way below and deeper into the keep. Well, I have no further information. So lead on, my lord."

Behind the door, stone steps led down into darkness. Taking torches from the wall brackets, and leaving the prisoners under guard, they descended.

Vorduthe was trying to guess what they would find: an armory, no doubt; dormitories where he hoped most of the remaining garrison was sleeping at this moment; rest rooms, ablutions, a kitchen—perhaps an exercise and arms practice room, though the roof of the fortress was more likely used for that. Somewhere there would be comfortable quarters for the higher ranks—and for Mistirea, if he was not kept in a dungeon. And there would have to be ample storerooms to enable the stronghold to stand alone for lengthy periods.

The place smelled dank. At first the torches revealed only a forest of squat pillars supporting a low ceiling. Then Vorduthe saw rows of barrels, and realized that this was a storage area. He lifted a lid. The barrel contained water.

Someone appeared at the limit of the flickering torchlight. It was a large Peldainian, clad not in a white surplice but a hastily donned heavy cuirass, laces dangling untied, a helmet in his hand.

"What means this noise?" he called. "What's amiss?"

Vorduthe motioned to Lord Korbar, who swept forward. "Nothing to concern you anymore," the noble answered. He thrust quickly with his sword, and the Peldainian toppled.

But others were behind him, having emerged, probably, from their quarters. Vorduthe snapped an order, and joined in the rush on the strangers. There were cries of anger and disbelief, and a clash of metal.

The encounter was brief. Several Peldainians were killed within seconds by the ferocious serpent harriers. Others fled into the darkness and some, all avenues of escape cut off, threw down their weapons and begged for mercy.

"Hold!" called Vorduthe, aware that in their present mood his men might massacre the entire garrison if not restrained. "Troop Leader Kana-Kem, see that these prisoners are added to those above, then return to help in the search. Winkling out every Peldainian in this warren might take some time."

He did not wait to see this done. The Arelians fanned out in small groups. Detailing one serpent harrier to accompany him, he first examined a nearby cramped dormitory, the place from which the Peldainians they had just confronted must have come. He could almost feel pity for men who had been roused from their sleep to have to face the fiercest warriors on Thelessa.

There was no stealth now, but noise from every direction. The stronghold was being cleared out with enthusiasm. Neither was it so dark: the men had lit wall-cressets as they went. Vorduthe found a stairwell which took him down one more level. Here the wall-cressets were already lit, and the air was fresher, probably ventilated.

The foot of the stair was in the corner of two corridors. Vorduthe looked up one branch, saw no one, then turned his attention to the other—and froze.

Lord Korbar was approaching, presumably having preceded him or else having found another way down. Some paces behind him, Octrago followed. But in the instant that Vorduthe saw them, a Peldainian sprang on Korbar from ambush.

Octrago saw this too, but did not shout a warning; instead, an unmistakable look of calculation came to his eyes, and, it seemed to Vorduthe, he held back while the assailant plunged home a dagger.

Too late Vorduthe yelled and started forward. Octrago too now acted, seemingly spurred on by the realization of Vorduthe's presence. Running a few quick steps, he brushed aside the dagger which the assassin had yanked from Korbar's side, and ran his sword-point expertly through his heart.

Uttering scarcely a groan, the ambusher flopped across the body of his victim. Vorduthe knelt, pushed him away, then gently turned Korbar on his back. The Arelian noble's eyes flickered. He looked dully at Vorduthe.

"I scarcely knew where the thrust came from, my lord," he whispered.

His eyes became empty. He was dead.

Vorduthe stood. He stared with open hostility at Octrago.

"You could have saved him," he accused harshly.

"Not so, my lord Vorduthe," Octrago murmured apologetically. "The attack took me by surprise . . . I confess my mind was elsewhere."

Vorduthe hesitated. It was difficult to prove or even to know for certain. Yet Octrago could have seen a decided advantage in getting rid of Korbar, his severest critic and even enemy.

"I am sincerely sorry for the death of your fellow nobleman, and, I am sure, personal friend," Octrago said in a conciliatory tone. "Many have died in this enterprise. And who knows that we may not be next?"

Vorduthe bit his lip. He would have to let his doubts override his anger, he realized . . . it was possible that Octrago was telling the truth.

But he would not forget this moment.

Korbar's killer had emerged from behind a hanging screen which covered a short section of wall, and which Octrago now slid aside. It hid a recess, and in the recess was a narrow door.

"I'll warrant that man was a guard . . ." Octrago suggested. He tried the latch of the door. If there were bolts on the inside, they were not fastened, for the door swung open.

Sword before him, Vorduthe entered, his gaze flicking first to his left, then, seeing no ambush from that quarter, he stepped smartly to one side and swung the door partly to.

No one was behind it. The chamber was well furnished. Its only occupant was an elderly man seated at a desk facing the door. He held raised in both hands a dagger, which he pointed at his own heart.

The old man was lean, vigorous-looking for his age, and had lank white hair. He wore a long robe, with the same image of tree and pool as was worn by the others stitched on the chest.

The glint of determination in his eyes turned to perplexity when he saw Vorduthe. He was puzzled by his foreign appearance, Vorduthe thought.

But his expression changed to one of recognition when Octrago entered, and his grasp on the knife handle firmed. Vorduthe ordered the serpent harrier to stand guard outside, then looked questioningly at the Peldainian by whose guidance he had come so far.

Octrago nodded in confirmation. "It is he. Mistirea, High Priest of the Lake." He raised his voice, addressing the old man. "Why do you not bid me welcome, Mistirea?"

The priest's gaze flicked from one man to the other. His hold on the knife did not waver. "I shall destroy myself instantly if forced against my will. Who is this peculiar stranger you bring, and how did you enter the castle?"

"Why, we came by the back way, High Priest. Over the sea, and through the forest. And this is Lord Vorduthe, who helped bring me here. He is from a land beyond the ocean. If you do not believe me, ask him yourself. And now you must come with us."

It gave Vorduthe an eerie sensation to hear Mistirea speak in the same sharp, mangled accent that Octrago himself used. "What he says is true," he told the old man. "We have brought you back your rightful monarch, King Askon."

Mistirea gazed at Octrago with an expression it was impossible to read.

Octrago answered with his familiar wry smile. "Much has happened, and there is much that I shall have to explain to you. I beseech you to put down your knife, old man. You are to return with us to the lake."

"There is much, perhaps, that should be explained to me," Vorduthe said in a low tone. "I had thought Mistirea a prisoner in this place. But perhaps he is now your prisoner, instead."

"The High Priest has duties to perform," Octrago said, his voice acid. "Duties essential to the well-being of the realm, but which he has neglected for some time. Was that by your own choice, Mistirea? It is a question that torments us."

It seemed that Mistirea's eyes also became tormented as Octrago said this. But he put down the knife and rose to his feet.

Moving round the desk, he turned his attention to Vorduthe, who noticed now, as the loose robe flowed over his shoulders, how unusually well-muscled those shoulders were for a man of his age. He looked Vorduthe directly in the eye, the misery Vorduthe had briefly thought to see gone from his gaze. Instead his stare was penetrating and sharp.

In fact, Vorduthe found the pale blue eyes frightening. "You have done well, King Askon," Mistirea said in a suddenly strong voice. "Doubly well, to bring this stranger to our land."

Intently he studied Vorduthe's face, then let his gaze travel over his body. "I have dreamed of such a man," he murmured. "Now, perhaps, my dream is answered."

There was silence. Octrago, Vorduthe noticed, was frowning in discomfiture or mystification. He did not seem to know what Mistirea was talking about, any more than Vorduthe himself did.

"In truth I am not my lord Vorduthe's monarch," Octrago said smoothly at last. "He has a monarch in his own land, to whom a reward is due greater than anything you may expect, Mistirea. But enough of that for the moment. There is only one issue to be settled. Do you return home with us and resume your duties, or must we force you to it, *by whatever means are necessary?*"

Mistirea's broad shoulders sagged a little. Then he raised his head defiantly.

"I have laid down the dagger, have I not? By that I signified that I will accompany you. What happens at the lake . . . well, we shall see. . . ."

"Yes, we shall see that what must be done *is* done," Octrago said tightly. Stepping forward, he picked up the dagger. "One of my lord Vorduthe's men will stay by you till morning, to see you do not change your mind. A dead High Priest is no use to Peldain."

"Wait!" Vorduthe said. "You have not settled with me."

He faced Mistirea and spoke coolly. "We have come a long way, High Priest, at your king's behest, and I require information. The men in this place are acolytes of your cult and wear the same badge as yourself. Furthermore, King Askon seems prepared to take you as his prisoner rather than a rescued friend. So what were you up until now—this stronghold's prisoner, or its master?"

"Both," Mistirea replied somberly.

Octrago uttered a caustic laugh. "To that question I too would like a sensible answer, friend Vorduthe," he said. "As you have seen, I cannot obtain one. It is a secret Mistirea will not divulge. No matter. We are halfway to our purpose."

He sighed. "Now with your permission, my lord, let us see if all the crannies in this heap of stone have been cleared."

Chapter Ten

For all of the following day Vorduthe's force remained in possession of the stronghold, having slain half its garrison and taken the rest prisoner. The men rested, and chose additional weapons from the captured armory—daggers, lances, bows and quiversful of arrows. Broken-up furniture provided sufficient timber to build a funeral pyre for Lord Korbar and the two dead serpent harriers. The ceremony was held on the fortress roof, and while the smoke rose to the sky the men gathered round, asking anxious questions.

"What are our prospects, my lord?" Donatwe Mankas, a troop leader, pressed Vorduthe. "Our numbers are negligible and the Peldainians in this castle, at least, were not without fighting skill. We alone could not conquer a whole country."

Octrago was elsewhere in the fortress and Vorduthe was expected to speak frankly. Yet it was difficult to be hopeful. A sad vision had come to his mind. He pictured the fleet from the Hundred Islands returning to the landing place,

waiting at anchor a few days, then departing with
the news that the expedition had failed to appear.
No one—not King Krassos, not Vorduthe's wife,
nor any Arelian—would ever know what had become of the costly army that had so bravely set
forth.

He motioned the men closer, and spoke while
the flames flickered on his face. "We cannot go
back, we can only go forward to whatever the
gods have in store for us. But in one respect
matters lie in our favor. We have in our possession both the claimant to the throne and the high
priest of this country, and that may well be worth
a thousand armed men."

He paused before continuing. "I sense much
underhandedness in the way the Peldainians con-
duct their affairs—Octrago and Mistirea, at any
rate, are hard to pin down. Now we are blunt
soldiers and strangers to deviousness. But one
thing we can resolve—we serve King Krassos to
the last, and if Askon Octrago betrays us he dies,
king or no."

That was his last word on the subject and he
ordered the men back to work, preparatory to
their departure next day. It would have been im-
practicable to take prisoners on the march, so he
set about stripping the fortress of its weapons.
The catapults were smashed, and the boulders
that were stored in the stones-chute sent rattling
down the cliff face. It would take some time, he
reckoned, to fill it again.

He also dealt with the poisonous vapor that
was contained, it developed, in the barrels stacked

in the first storeroom he had entered. It was stored in the form of a horrid jelly which had to be burned in the vats in the forecourt, so as to give off a dense deadly smoke that flowed to the lowest level.

Octrago offered the information that the jelly was derived from a tree resin. "Nearly everything in Peldain comes from a tree," he smiled. "Only stones and metal come from anything else."

Vorduthe recalled the furniture he had seen, with its grainy, rough-finished quality. He had inspected Mistirea's desk, for instance. It almost seemed to have grown into shape, for he had not found a single join. He guessed it had been carved from a single piece of wood, carefully chosen by some patient craftsman.

"You are cut off from the sea here," he remarked. "Many of our materials come from ocean life."

He ordered the barrels rolled farther along the cliff, and their smelly contents poured over the edge.

Early next morning the war party wound its way down the big newel that was drilled through the interior of the cliff. At the bottom was a short tunnel whose exit was barred by a massive slab of stone. This was raised by means of an ingenious counterbalance, and they walked out into daylight.

Here it was even more striking how absolutely the fortress dominated the region. The path along the foot of the cliff was no more than a narrow ledge. It bordered a drear swamp stretching as far as the eye could see, plentifully dotted with trees, or possibly they were only bushes, of a squat, splayed appearance. Vorduthe thought them sinister enough to avoid at all cost, even had the swamp not been impossibly marshy.

Seeing him scan the terrain, Octrago smiled his understanding. "The bog is deep," he said. "Nothing would get through it, not even a boat. And yes, those bog-trees are death to touch, although they don't compare in deadliness with the trees of the forest. They are sticky-trees—even a bird that alights on one never gets away. Still, we needn't worry about that."

He pointed to a narrow swath of firm ground that divided the swamp in two, extending from near where they stood to the horizon. It was raised slightly above the general level, and was marked at intervals by rough stone pillars. Vorduthe guessed it was an old causeway.

But why had it ever been laid? Ultimately the trail led over the mountain pass and to the strip of open land lying between the Clear Peaks and the forest—too small a territory to be worth a major feat of engineering, notwithstanding the sculpted hill. Still less did it seem worth building a mountain fortress to guard the route.

The arrangement would make more sense if larger territories to the east were the intended destination. But on the map of the island Octrago had drawn back in Arelia, eastern Peldain was entirely given over to the forest, with only the Clear Peaks themselves free.

They moved away from the tunnel entrance.

Suddenly there were startled yells from a number of serpent harriers, who had looked up to view the castle overhead. An avalanche of human bodies was tumbling down the cliff face. They crunched sickeningly on the rock pathway, spattering it with blood and leaving it piled with smashed limbs.

"They are disposing of their dead," Vorduthe said grimly. "Expedience is all, apparently."

The war party set off in good order along the causeway. Octrago and Mistirea marched side by side, the High Priest wearing a purple cloak. Vorduthe stayed close by them to eavesdrop on any conversation, but either they had nothing to say to one another or they were wary of speaking in his presence.

As time went by the rotten, sulfurous smell of the bog became overpowering. Occasionally huge armored beasts, their long snouts crammed with teeth, broke surface and regarded the travelers with beady eyes. But only once did one of the monsters heave itself onto the causeway to confront them, and it was soon driven off using lances.

Before the sun had reached its height the party had crossed the swamp and the land began to alter in character. The ground was sometimes mossy, sometimes grassy, much as in the forest except that trees grew only in rare clumps and seemed entirely innocuous.

The sun shone strongly and behind them the tips of the Clear Peaks were still visible, shining whitely. A change of mood had come over Octrago. He smiled often, and became relaxed. Suddenly, to the immense surprise of all the Arelians, he began to sing—a flowing song in an alien scale, with words which, though they were sung in their common tongue, Vorduthe could not fathom.

At midday they halted to eat and drink of the supplies taken from the castle. Vorduthe sat with the Peldainians, some way apart from the others.

"It is time we outlined our strategy," he said.

"Indeed we have need of very little," Octrago said good-humoredly. "In two days or less we shall be in Lakeside."

He was speaking of the capital of Peldain which lay close to the sacred lake, though as far as Vorduthe could make out it was less of a town than Arcaiss, for instance. Indeed the mode of life of the Peldainians was something still to be clarified.

"And there you still intend to claim the throne from your cousin Kestrew?"

"With your assistance, yes," Octrago answered, with a glance at Mistirea.

"You are returning with no larger a force than you left with," Vorduthe reminded him. "How much resistance may we expect between here and Lakeside? And how much support can you rally to your cause?"

"We shall meet virtually no resistance, but neither shall we receive support," Octrago informed him. "My face will not be familiar in the villages along the way, and I shall preserve my anonymity. As I have explained, there is no standing army in Peldain, and with luck news of our coming will reach Lakeside no faster than we shall get there."

"You say Peldain is not a warrior country, yet that is not the impression I received in the mountain fortress," Vorduthe commented.

"Fighting skills are preserved among the acolytes of the cult, traditionally to protect the High Priest, and the nobility learn swordsmanship mainly for sport. You can form your own view as to how the acolytes performed as compared with your own men. And my cousin Kestrew will no doubt have gathered a band of ruffians about himself. How great an adversary that will present at this stage is hard to say. Do not despair—we have two great advantages. We have a band of disciplined fighting men—my previous followers could not really claim to be that. And perhaps even more important, we have the High Priest."

"And where was Mistirea at the time of your departure?" Vorduthe asked.

Mistirea kept his eyes downcast and did not speak. "He had already taken himself off to the retreat in the mountains, probably to avoid the civil disorder, or else to avoid taking sides," Octrago said dryly, and Mistirea did not gainsay him.

"If everything you say is true, he could probably have decided the issue and saved you much trouble," Vorduthe observed. He pondered. "Tell me about this religion of yours. What gods do you worship? And what is the significance of the lake, 'the eye of Peldain,' as you call it?"

Octrago looked at the High Priest as though expecting him to answer. But Mistirea only made a small gesture indicating that he should speak.

"The lake has more than one title," Octrago said to Vorduthe. It is known as 'the eye of Peldain' because the human eye is like a pool that reflects the soul, and so the phrase really refers to its surface. In the depths of the lake dwells the soul of Peldain. That is our god, if you like, but it has no other name.

"The High Priest has a special duty. He must regularly dive into the lake and commune with the presence there. Only he can do this, for only he is familiar with the spirit. By this propitiation the affairs of the realm are kept in good order. If it is not done, or not done successfully, all will be chaos. Peldain will be destroyed."

"And the populace believes this?"

"Absolutely."

Vorduthe nodded. This he could understand. Superstitious beliefs were a reality for the less sophisticated inhabitants of the Hundred Islands, too.

"Then the absence of Mistirea is cause for considerable unease, I imagine."

"You are correct. And there lies our strength."

Continuing, they found themselves walking through open countryside with no hint of a road or trail. The air became warm and balmy, the scenery like some other-worldly paradise with numerous little lakes and streams, strange trees and plants.

Habitations also came in sight, in the form of hutlike houses, always accompanied by a small grove of the unfamiliar trees, of which there seemed to be an extensive variety. Human figures were also sometimes visible, watching the passing procession with curiosity, but Octrago ignored them.

He kept well away from any houses until, near the end of the day, they came to a fair-sized village. At first Vorduthe did not recognize it as such and thought they had entered a spacious wood in which people walked. But, spread out between the trees, there were dwellings of various kinds.

"Do not announce me," Octrago warned the Hundred Islanders. "Remember, I am incognito."

At the column's approach the villagers drew back, though they seemed more bewildered than afraid. Mistirea broke ranks and stepped toward them, raising his hands in greeting.

"Do not fear, good people. These men are not here to work you any harm."

"It is the High Priest!" someone exclaimed wonderingly.

"Have you returned to us?" pleaded another.

Vorduthe wondered why Mistirea was recognizable while Octrago, a claimant to the throne, was not. Then he remembered that the High Priest's cloak bore the identifying cult emblem. He might, even, be a more famous personage than Octrago.

"Will all now be set right?" a middle-aged woman in a purple gown asked anxiously.

Mistirea lowered his head. "I am here, am I not?"

A mood of relief and merriment flitted over the

gathering at these words. The villagers lost their
nervousness and flocked around the serpent harriers, but received only noncommital replies to
their questions as the warriors had been ordered.
Octrago led the way to a spacious arbor laid out
with tables and chairs. This, it turned out, was a
place of public relaxation where refreshing drinks
were served. As many of the soldiery as could
found places in its shade; the rest settled themselves on the moss outside.

A beaker made of a very hard and shiny dark-
brown wood was set before Vorduthe. From a
large green gourd was poured a cool amber liquid.

He drank, and found the delicious fluid running down his throat almost of its own volition.
It had a tangy, acid flavor that was quite irresistible.

Octrago laughed, then quenched his own thirst.
Vorduthe idly examined the beaker. It was a fine
piece of work, its polish brilliant and perfect,
with only one blemish on the outside of the handle. It must have taken many hours of work to
produce.

"You have expert craftsmen here in Peldain,"
he remarked.

"Craftsmen? We have very few craftsmen at all."

Octrago pointed through the open side of the
arbor to one of the smaller trees growing just
outside it. At first Vorduthe did not know what
he was trying to show him. Then, looking closer
at the tree, he suffered a shock of understanding.

Hanging from the tree, after the manner of fruit,
were dozens of beakers identical to the one he
had just drunk from.

Octrago again laughed to see his astonishment. "My lord, some facts relating to my country I confess I have not told you. In Arelia it was a matter of amazement to me to see how much labor was involved in everyday life. Practically ever item of use had to be painstakingly made by hand—even providing food cost endless time spent in cultivating or fishing.

"Here life is more commodious. Know, my lord, that the interior of Peldain is a garden where human needs are all provided by nature. Look about you. Our trees give us more than our food and drink. Clothing, utensils and dwellings all are grown for us by some type of tree or other. That beaker you just drank from, the platters on which our supper is shortly to be served, the table and chairs we are using—all are grown to shape by our trees. Even the knife to cut your food is tree grown, complete to its edge of tough wood."

He pointed to the blemish on the beaker's handle. "See, that is where it was plucked from the branch."

Vorduthe looked at the beaker again, then at the table. He remembered Mistirea's desk in the castle.

"*Clothing?*" he echoed.

"Well, only the simplest garments are actually grown complete and to size. The clothing trees produce fabrics in shapes which may be easily stitched together. Observe, they are of excellent quality. It is easier than weaving grasses, is it not?"

The garments worn by the village Peldainians were not elaborate: loose tunics and breeches for the men, simple flowing gowns for the women. Only two colors were represented: purple and green. That trees could produce the silky material, perhaps as the lining of pods, was not hard to grasp.

That rough furniture might be cut from suitably selected trees was also comprehensible. But the furniture he had seen was anything but rough. And household utensils? The vision of the green-leafed tree yonder was beyond belief. More credible would have been if the beakers had been tied in place as a piece of trickery.

As for houses . . . Vorduthe let his gaze wander to the dwellings within view. They were tidy little cottages, some with several rooms, solid and shapely.

"They are obtained thus-wise," Octrago said when Vorduthe questioned him. "A single house-tree grows only one room—though the type of room differs according to variety. The trunk develops a hollow, then expands and takes the shape of walls, floor and roof. Doors and windows develop, the doors on bark hinges and the windows filming over with transparent resin. When mature, the trunk's connection with the root withers. The leaf-bearing branches also fall off. It may then be moved to wherever it is needed. If several rooms are placed together they bond into one structure in a few days, and the rooms also root themselves to the ground. Meanwhile, the roots left behind generate new trees."

"So no one has to work," Vorduthe said, as he mulled over Octrago's extraordinary revelation.

"Not as people in the Hundred Islands work. Life here is pleasant and easy-going. You will soon grow accustomed to it."

Vorduthe grunted, far from pleased by the suggestion. Though he had never thought the three or four hours worked per day by most islanders particularly arduous, it was what distinguished civilized life from the habits of primitives, who before coming under the rule of Arelia had preferred to laze around all day and would not work at all unless forced to it.

A more disciplined sense of social organization would doubtless be of benefit here, he thought.

"But you have some craftsmen, I presume."

"We have metal-workers. The craft goes by family and brings great esteem. But there are not many such. Also there are a few people who work in stone, but not nearly as many as in ages past when the mountain stronghold was built."

"Someone must tend these marvelous trees. Indeed, someone must have bred them in the first place."

Octrago shook his head. "They have always been here, and no one tends them. They are a natural feature of the country."

That was not possible, Vorduthe told himself. They could only be the result of some extraordinary art of tree culture practiced in a forgotten past. It was peculiar to hear a man of Octrago's intelligence aver otherwise.

"Is there not a drawback to being so dependent

on nature?" he said. "How many different kinds of appurtenance can the trees produce? What if a new type of utensil is wanted? It would not be available."

"Almost anything can be provided," Octrago said with a smile. "It will sound strange to you, but the trees are sensitive to our thoughts. If something new or different is needed, then after a while—a quarter of a year, perhaps—a tree begins to grow it."

"Incredible," Vorduthe muttered.

"Even weapons," Octrago added. "We have trees to grow bows and arrows."

"You do? Just the same, I can see why you say Peldain should be easy to conquer. People who are not used to hard work do not fight well. They become soft."

He brooded. There was something almost sinister in this idea of trees which responded to thought and thereby sustained an entire society. He felt an urge not only to find a way of wiping out the coastal forest but to cut down every other tree as well, if he managed to gain possession of the country.

But he was forgetting. King Askon would be ruler, subject only to the will of King Krassos.

Well, there might eventually be room for much alteration there.

The villagers were mingling with the seaborne warriors, who had begun to take liberties with the young women, to the displeasure both of parents and the young men of the village. Vorduthe intervened before there was bloodshed—his men were in no mood to tolerate hostility. Once they were fed, with a generous hospitality he now realized was no more than normal behavior here, he separated them. Not far away was a pleasant pool, fed by a clear stream, which the villagers used for bathing. He ordered the men there, so they could wash away the sweat and grime of their long ordeal.

It was an opportunity every man used with enthusiasm, including himself. After he had enjoyed himself in the water he returned to the bank where he had left his weapons, armor and garments. He found Mistirea standing there, watching him sharply.

"You swim well," the Peldainian High Priest remarked.

Vorduthe grinned. "Everyone in the Hundred Islands swims well."

"Of course. Here it is not a necessary attainment . . . for most. Can you dive?"

"Naturally."

"How deep? How long can you stay under?"

"Long enough to find pink shells in the coral shallows," said Vorduthe, still grinning. Mistirea frowned. Shells and coral were foreign words to him.

Suddenly he stripped off the purple cloak he wore, followed by the shiftlike robe beneath it. Naked, he stood on the edge of the pool, and Vorduthe could now see more clearly how magnificently muscled he was about the shoulders and torso.

With barely a pause the old man plunged into the water, then swam strongly to the middle of the pool, keeping his distance from others who still disported there. It was evident he was a much-practiced swimmer. He floated for a moment, then flipped himself over and disappeared beneath the surface.

Vorduthe kept his eye on the center of the expanding ripples where he had been. Time passed; the ripples smoothed over. More time passed. He scanned the pool: Mistirea had nowhere reappeared.

Alarmed now, he called to the serpent harriers in the pool, urging them to dive in search of the missing priest. As they were about to obey him Mistirea suddenly surfaced, in the exact spot from which he had vanished. He spent a moment or two filling his lungs. Then, still swimming easily with vigorous strokes, he returned to the bank to stand before Vorduthe.

"Can you stay down that long?" he demanded.

". . . I am not sure," Vorduthe confessed.

"You will dive. You will dive deep and long."

To his vast surprise the dripping High Priest placed both hands on Vorduthe's shoulders and stared with an almost insane intensity into his eyes.

"You are Peldain's salvation," he said in a low, urgent tone. "I and I alone am able to recognize you, and this I know."

His hands dropped. He stooped to retrieve his garments, then turned and strode away, leaving Vorduthe gazing after him in bemusement.

Chapter Eleven

Several times during the night Vorduthe and Octrago were called on to intervene in disturbances where the serpent harriers, conscious of past and coming dangers, recklessly sought to enjoy themselves with the village's women. It was a sullen set of local folk who early next morning gave the strangers a filling breakfast of crunchy nut-flavoured cobs, quite unlike any fruit they had ever seen, and with relief bade them farewell.

The day proved idyllic. The Hundred Islanders marched leisurely through an enchanted landscape carpeted with the soft mosses and waving grasses of Peldain. There were clear streams, hillocks, villages and hamlets—always set amid groves of the magical trees that gave the country its magical economy.

They met no resistance, and Vorduthe began to wonder if the Peldainians were akin to savages, unable to organize themselves effectively or defend their territory.

"As we shall soon enter Lakeside, our strategy must be decided," he said to Octrago during the midday halt. "What is your intention?"

"First let me hear your proposals," Octrago countered.

"Well, do you think it is conceivable that a force like ours could actually take possession of the kingdom? If the center is seized, is all done? And can the center in fact be seized?"

"It is the same here as in the Hundred Islands," Octrago told him. "Strength is what counts. The difference is that here one needs little strength, since the opposition has little. Very well, then. Come, I will draw a map of Lakeside. We shall infiltrate by night and converge on the king's palace. There we shall give Kestrew and his band of ruffians their desserts. Tomorrow morning Mistirea will proclaim me king—and you will deal with dissenters, first of all in Lakeside and later throughout the land."

"This is easier than you made it sound in Arcaiss."

"There was the forest to deal with," Octrago said blandly.

Vorduthe became accusing. "So you admit deception."

"Deception? No, more a case of altered emphasis. One must marshal one's arguments carefully when speaking with kings. Arelians have a horror of Peldain's coastal forest. Overcoming that horror was my first difficulty."

"Clearly you have some kingcraft yourself,"

Vorduthe said bitterly. It was hard not to feel hatred when he thought of his destroyed army.

"My motives were honorable."

While speaking, Octrago was sketching on a boulder with a piece of sharp stone. "Here is the lake and here is the palace—though 'palace' is your word. We call it the king's tree. The approaches are through these avenues, thus and thus—it is straightforward enough. I will draw this map again when I find a convenient piece of tree bark, and your men can all study it. What do you think?"

"How many armed men may we expect to find within?"

"That I cannot say. Neither do I know whether Kestrew will have any stationed on guard round about, but no doubt we can find out. At any rate I am certain your men will give a good account of themselves."

"How shall we find out about the guards? By sending scouts?"

Octrago sucked his lower lip thoughtfully. "I will go into Lakeside ahead of you. I must take Mistirea into a place of safety among friends. There I will make inquiries, and return to you."

With a sour smile Vorduthe shook his head. "You and the High Priest remain with us. You are our guarantee that all is as you say."

"How sad to find you so distrusting," Octrago sighed. "I hope this mood will disappear when we rule Peldain together."

"I am sure it will since, as you agreed with

King Krassos, I shall have military command. You must then trust me."

"Well, I know you for an honorable man," Octrago murmured.

Contemplating the coming action, Vorduthe realized that the whole enterprise would now hang on one stroke.

Still, that was the kind of situation he liked.

Late in the day the terrain began to rise and to break up into a region of knolls and ridges. It was a bare and dusty landscape interspersed with clumps of verdure. Octrago led the party up a ridge and into a curious wood, the like of which they had never seen.

The trees were small, like Arelia's fruit trees, but were twisted, seeming to writhe, and were bleached in color, seemingly without bark. The tortured, convoluted branches all joined up overhead and seemed a single network, and greenery grew only on the topmost part.

It was like walking under a low, vaulted ceiling carved by an insane mason. To Vorduthe, the sight resembled nothing so much as an enormous exposed brain.

Remembering the forest, the men were nervous until they assured themselves that the trees of this wood, however weird in appearance, were as still and passive as any in Arelia. Vorduthe, however, could not avoid an oppressive feeling, and he noticed that the men became subdued and quiet.

Glancing at him, Octrago paused and leaned

with one hand against a tree trunk that was like a column of frozen wriggles. He let his gaze wander over the elaborate canopy.

"This is called Cog Wood," he informed in a distant tone. "You feel it, don't you? I can see it on your face."

"Feel what?" Vorduthe asked him.

"Its presence. I told you before that the trees can hear our thoughts. Now, if you are quiet in your mind, you may hear this wood's thoughts. Yes, it thinks—after a fashion. These wooden sinews—" he gestured to the overhead twisted branches—"are the cranial channels of a kind of brain. Tree touches tree and branch joins branch so that they become as it were one tree. Do you not hear it thinking?"

"No," Vorduthe said, but he was half-lying. There *was* a feeling of presence, as though the wood were alive and watching, and it was an oppressive feeling.

Octrago, however, seemed in no hurry to leave the place. He sauntered between the narrow trunks, looking about him as though attempting to attune himself to the vegetable mentality he claimed existed—a claim Vorduthe could not take seriously, especially considering the beliefs of the cult Mistirea represented.

They came atop the ridge, descended a series of terrace-like depressions, then broke from the tree cover.

Below them lay Lakeside, spread out on land that sloped very gently to the east. Half wood, half town, the buildings merged with the trees almost without distinction. From Octrago's rough map Vorduthe recognized the king's tree, or palace—a large construction, probably of several stories, bedecked with verandahs and, in a gorgeous display, broad-leaved branches.

To the east of the town was the lake, irregularly shaped, its east shore sustained by raised banks. The oddest thing about it was its color: not blue, or grayish like some muddied waters, but distinctly green, so that it seemed at first like a discoloration on the spread moss.

For what remained of daylight they remained on the slopes overlooking the town, keeping out of sight. Night came, and the massed stars appeared, making the lake gleam unnaturally.

"The eye of Peldain watches the stars," Octrago said at Vorduthe's elbow, after the manner of one quoting a familiar saying.

"And what does the soul of Peldain do?" Vorduthe replied ironically.

"Broods, perhaps."

The men had been briefed and each was aware of what he had to do. The party swarmed down the slope, spreading out so as to move through the town in twos and threes. No street lamps burned on stone pedestals as would have been the case in Arcaiss—the Peldainians retired early. In fact there were no proper streets, only footworn paths between the houses, from whose resined windows came soft light and the sound of voices.

They met no one on their way to the big building that was the palace. Inspecting it at closer quarters, Vorduthe paused to wonder if such an elaborate structure really could have been jig-sawed together from individually grown units, as the larger Peldainian dwellings usually were. It seemed barely possible. Perhaps, he thought, it had been grown *in situ* as the conjoined product of a grove of trees—or perhaps it even resulted from a single gargantuan tree.

Octrago whispered nervously. "Mistirea should wait out here. We cannot risk the life of the High Priest."

"We are all at risk," Vorduthe retorted. "He comes with us."

Theirs was the largest group, numbering eight, the reason being that they had also surreptitiously to guard Mistirea and Octrago. Around the palace, metal glinted in the starlight. The others were moving into position.

So far there had been no challenge and no guards stood at the foliage's entrance, though the many windows glowed with light. Vorduthe advanced into the open and raised his arm as a signal. Seaborne warriors flitted to the large ground windows.

A double-panelled door on thick leatherlike hinges, patterned like a gnarled tree, blocked the entrance. It creaked open easily when Vorduthe pushed it, and he slipped inside, motioning to the others to follow.

The broad hallway in which they stood could almost have been the interior of a spacious building in Arcaiss, were it not for the alienness of the designs on the walls. Vorduthe was used to carved wood and bright, simple colors. The soft, full light came from numerous cressets. Opposite the door a staircase, organically grown like everything else, led to a balcony or gallery.

The place was empty of Peldainians. Cracking sounds came from nearby. The seaborne warriors were breaking the windows, as quietly as they could, and filtering into the palace. Finding no resistance, they gathered together, looking to Vorduthe for guidance.

Suddenly a serpent harrier uttered a warning exclamation, pointing with his sword. Vorduthe whirled in time to see Octrago and Mistirea disappearing through a small door to the right of the stairway. Three of the men who were to have watched them charged in pursuit, but the door slammed and held as they tried to force it.

"Sorry, my lord," another said. "They caught us unawares."

"Too late now—don't waste time on them." Vorduthe raised his voice. "Spread through the palace, put down any and all resistance as you find it." He picked out a group of men. "You come with me. The rest—that way, and that."

He was about to mount the stairway, when men appeared on the gallery.

They were Peldainians, their bony white faces peering down curiously but without fear at the invaders. They were garbed for combat, carrying swords and timber shields, and wearing breastplates and helmets of honey-colored metal. All this Vorduthe perceived in a moment, for in that instant what he had taken to be a ceiling decora-

tion detached itself from the ceiling and fell on
the whole gathering of Arelians.

It was a net. Like the others, Vorduthe tried to
cut his way through it with his sword, but this
was no ordinary net. It was not made of rope. Its
flexions reminded him of triproot or stranglevine,
except that it acted not to strangle or to amputate
but only to immobilise. And this it did by pro-
gressive squeezing. Swords fell from nerveless
hands; arms quivered with the effort to break free
as the net wrapped itself tighter, embracing each
man individually.

The net was a living thing that reacted to movement, even the movement of breathing. Vorduthe
realized this belatedly. He held his breath in an
attempt to fool the net, but it remembered its
victim, and whenever he breathed out a little it
contracted around his thorax, preventing him from
drawing breath again.

Suffocation overwhelmed him, vision faded.
With a faint croak of frustration, Vorduthe lost
consciousness.

With hands hauling him to his feet, he knew he
had not been out for long. The net had been
drawn back and was rolled up against the wall.
The bony-faced men in honey armor were everywhere, dragging and herding the disarmed Arelians
to one side with cuffs, blows and pricks with
swordpoints.

The voice of Troop Leader Kana-Kem cried out
hoarsely. "*Remember our pledge, Commander!
Remember!*"

Vorduthe felt shame. He had led his men into a trap.

Before he could reply, another voice called out.

"That man must be kept apart from the others!"

It came from Mistirea. Vorduthe raised his eyes and saw four figures descending the staircase. The High Priest was pointing to Vorduthe, and Octrago was by his side.

With them was a man very advanced in years who stepped carefully with the aid of a stick, watched over by an accompanying servant. He wore a robe of a glowing lilac color laced with silver, more sumptuous than anything Vorduthe had yet seen in Arelia. The skin of his face was like bone bleached and weathered on the beach. Yet except for its age, even taking national likeness into account, it was remarkably like Octrago's.

The four stopped a few steps from the floor. There was a sudden silence, and the guards paused in their work to bow to the old man, who inspected everything with a kind of bewildered interest.

Vorduthe would have expected a roar of rage from the seaborne warriors at the entrance of Octrago. Instead they were as still as statues, and as silent, only their eyes betraying their feelings.

"This trap has been well laid," Vorduthe announced loudly. "Your talent for treachery now becomes evident, Askon Octrago—tell me, is this your cousin Kestrew, the false king we were to turn off the throne? If so, why are we prisoners and you are not?"

The old man gave a puzzled look to Octrago, who twisted his mouth in a cynical smile.

"There is no cousin Kestrew," he told Vorduthe. He sounded almost sad. "That was a tale I spun to serve my purpose. But as for treachery, I want you to understand that everything I have done I did for the sake of my country. And since you ask, you see before you King Kerenei, undisputed monarch of Peldain—whose eldest son I am."

Vorduthe's head swam with this news. "Korbar was right all along," he muttered. "Everything has been lies. . . ."

"Nearly everything."

For the first time the old king spoke, quaveringly. "Askon, what should be done with these strangers?"

Octrago did not reply instantly. He looked pensively at Vorduthe, who held the gaze, and it seemed that his supercilious expression softened slightly.

"They must all be put to death, father, and immediately. Perhaps I could wish it otherwise, but they are hopeful fools whom I have led a long way from home and used to good purpose. They will be dangerous to us while they live."

Were it not for the guards who held him Vorduthe would have hurled himself at Octrago's throat, but instead it was Mistirea who intervened. He swept past Octrago, pointing to Vorduthe.

"If you kill this man, Peldain dies with him!"

"The High Priest suddenly develops a conscience," Octrago said caustically. He spoke out of the corner of his mouth. "Give the order now, father, before my nerve breaks too."

Mistirea addressed himself imploringly to Kerenei. "Will no one listen to me? I am High Priest of the Lake no longer!"

"This is preposterous," Octrago drawled. "Father, I did not go through unimaginable trials just to have our High Priest prove obstinate now. These are desperate times and if he will not cooperate— force him!"

"You may torture me unto death," Mistirea said calmly. "It will make no difference. Peldain is doomed unless my successor can be found. Why, when I retired to the mountains, could you find no one to take my place? It is because there is no Peldainian able and worthy to fill the role, and if providence had not sent us new blood the Cult of the Lake would have died with me. This I have known for a long time."

He turned, pointing his finger at Vorduthe again. "This man is your new High Priest. There can be no other." He cast darting glances around him. "Who will gainsay me? You, Prince Askon? Do you have mental insight, to look into a man and tell whether he has the power of communion? Yes, you have impossible bravery and extraordinary resourcefulness too—but you are not an initiate of the cult."

King Kerenei's look of incredulity had become more and more pained. He stamped his stick on the stair. "Enough! I can take no more! After all this time my son, whom I had thought lost on a gallant but hopeless enterprise, has returned to me. He has succeeded beyond all our dreams, and still matters are not right! I cannot bear it!'' He turned to mount the stairs. "Askon, look into this matter. Mistirea's knowledge must be our guide.''

"As you say, Father.''

While the King took his leave Octrago, author of Vorduthe's misfortunes, sauntered to him. Despite himself he was evidently intrigued by what Mistirea had said.

Vorduthe spoke stiffly. "Whatever you want from me will not be forthcoming if a single one of my men is harmed.''

"You are quick to seize a scrap of advantage. . . .'' Octrago fingered the hilt of the upward-pointing Arelian sword he still wore. A hint of friendliness reurned to his manner. "Well, we shall see what transpires.''

"I marvel that you are able to face me, after your behavior,'' Vorduthe said. "One thing baffles me. No travelers passed us on the way here. We watched you all the time. Yet you still managed to give warning of our approach.''

"Cog Wood,'' Octrago supplied curtly. "I told you it could sense, even think after a fashion. Did you not notice how I tarried there? I wanted the wood to convey our perturbing presence to one of Mistirea's sensitives here in Lakeside. From then on our movements were followed.'' He smiled. "Our land has held a number of surprises for you. And now, my lord, it seems I must explain what really has been happening since the day I landed in Arelia.''

Chapter Twelve

"The Forest of Peldain has existed for as long as anyone can remember, and so have the bountiful trees which provide us with all our needs."

Prince Askon Octrago filled a beaker with a light yellow liquid poured from a green gourd. He had changed his apparel and wore garments seemingly made of oversized flower petals of various colors, though on closer inspection the material was substantial enough. He slaked his thirst, filled the beaker again and handed it to Vorduthe to drink.

They were in a small room somewhere in the palace. Vorduthe sat in a wooden chair, watched over by two guards. On one side of a table Octrago sat, relaxed and casual. On the other sat Mistirea.

Vorduthe did not know where his men had been taken. But Mistirea, unexpectedly his ally, had extracted a promise from King Kerenei that they would not be harmed—yet.

"You can see why we, at least, never considered the forest an enemy," Octrago went on. "It was—and is—our defense against invasion from islands we vaguely knew lie across the sea. We have lived safely for generation after generation, inside that impenetrable coastal barrier.

"The forest, however, is ferocious in more ways than one. It has a prodigious capacity for change. It can develop new plants, new weapons, more swiftly than you could believe. And if left to itself it would spread to cover the whole island, extinguishing all other life."

While Octrago spoke, Mistirea's expression became more gloomy and he lowered his head. Octrago glanced at him before continuing.

"That has not happened because the forest has always been kept under control. I have told you something of the cult of the lake. You imagined that this concerned ceremonies which had to be performed if a superstitious populace was not to become agitated. Not so. The duties of the cult are real. That lake is no ordinary lake. It is not water. It is a spiritual presence. In its depths, the spirit of the forest truly dwells.

"To control the forest by communing with this spirit is the function of the High Priest. Only a rare individual can do this, and he is selected for training early in life. Yet this is the duty that High Priest Mistirea chose to betray!"

Octrago's voice became loud and angry. He cast flashing glances at Mistirea. "He ceased to dive into the lake or to exert himself in any way. Instead he withdrew to the mountain fastness with the larger part of his servitors, offering no explanation. Since his departure the forest has turned rogue. It is spreading and eventually will engulf all Peldain. Even the artifact trees are beginning to turn savage and mutate into wild forms—does this tale not prick your conscience, High Priest?"

Mistirea seemed close to weeping. He shook his head, not in answer but with an air of misery.

"Tell your tale, Prince Askon," he mumbled.

"I shall." Octrago turned back to Vorduthe, with a sour look. "If only there had been another able to act as High Priest all would have been well. But none of the remaining sensitives were able to appease the spirit in the lake—not even the one Mistirea was supposed to have been training as his successor. Two sensitives drowned trying.

"All appeals to Mistirea to return were ignored. Three times we tried to take the fortress by assault, with considerable loss of life. We began to think our ancient, beautiful land was doomed.

"Finally I decided upon a truly desperate enterprise. Peldain disposes itself thus: the eastern limb is all forest, which also spreads a coastal strip to north and south one hundred leevers deep on average."

"You told us thirty to forty leevers, and no more than twenty where we were to cross!" Vorduthe interjected indignantly.

"Not my largest lie, nor yet my smallest," Octrago conceded. "In fact, the distance from the coast to the point where the underground river may be reached is fifty leevers, so it is still a uniquely short crossing which moreover leads to the Valley of the Hill Maiden, and thence to the pass over the Clear Peaks. Impossible things are thought of when a realm is imperiled, and I began to contemplate the impossible: a passage through fifty leevers of forest so as to take the fortress from the rear. I don't know if you are aware of it, but the forest doesn't actually extend all the way round Peldain. The west coast is an escarpment that rises almost half as high as the Clear Peaks themselves, and then drops straight down into the sea. Such a cliff could never be scaled or climbed, but we succeeded, by means of an ingenious system of pulleys fastened one after the other into the cliff face, in lowering an expedition of rafts and three hundred men into the sea. The plan was to float round the coast to the entry point, and then attempt to penetrate the forest."

"Did you have fire engines?" Vorduthe asked him.

"No we had nothing of that sort," Octrago said somberly. "Just some knowledge of the forest. We would never have made it, of course, that is clear now, and in truth it was clear then."

"What happened to you?"

"We of Peldain have no knowledge of the ocean. We were unable to guide our rafts when faced with wind and current. We were swept out to sea and the rafts became separated. One by one my companions died. As far as I know I alone have survived.

"The rest you know. I was picked up by an Arelian ship and taken to Arcaiss. Then began my second great enterprise—by deceit and persuasion, to induce King Krassos to mount an expedition that *could* get men through the forest."

Octrago smiled crookedly as he said this, and Vorduthe felt he now understood all the irony that throughout had exuded from him.

In spite of the hatred he felt for the man, it was impossible not to be impressed by what he had dared, and accomplished.

"So you see, I owe everything to the brave men of Arelia, even though I was prepared to slaughter every last one of you once my object was achieved," the prince said lightly. "You can be proud of one thing. We are the only men, to my knowledge, ever to journey through the forest from end to end, and live."

Mistirea had surged to his feet and now stood wringing his hands, his face a mask of emotional torment. *"It is untrue!"* he protested. *"It is untrue!"*

For once Octrago seemed genuinely puzzled. Mistirea continued his outburst, in the same agonized tone. "You have it the wrong way round! It is not because I deserted my post that the forest has turned wild! Could I be so remiss, so uncaring? I had already lost control! That was why I left you!"

Briefly he covered his face. "I knew long ago that I was failing. The spirit no longer listened to me. I sent acolytes to north and east, and south over the Clear Peaks. They told me the forest was spreading. And I could not stop it.

"As for Inteke, who was to be my successor, he ceased to make contact with the spirit altogether. Neither did any of the other sensitives meet with any success. It became plain to me what was happening. Peldain has come to an end. We have lived too long within the aura of the lake, of the forest, of the whole land. It has absorbed our psyches to the extent that we can no longer influence it. Another mind was needed; a new, strong psyche that was independent of the soul of Peldain. In other words, we needed a stranger, brought in from outside.

"I tried to explain this to the king, but he would not listen. Unfortunately, Prince Askon, your father is senile. I then broke all protocols and tried to broach the matter with you. I had to be careful with my words, for to be too open would be to sacrifice my life."

"Yes, I do remember your telling me some nonsense," Octrago muttered. "I was not interested, of course—the sensitives are always too emotional and distraught. Besides—" he spoke for the benefit of Vorduthe— "this is Peldain, where nothing ever changes. Now that I have been in other lands where events move swiftly, it is more comprehensible to me." He raised his eyes questioningly to Vorduthe. "He . . .?"

"No one would help me," Mistirea said. "No one would listen. I and my acolytes unaided could not find our way across the sea; it needed the resources of a king. Therefore I withdrew, esconcing myself in the ancient mountain castle. I did this to force a crisis. I was trying to force the king to act and do as I had advised.

"Now it seems my words were still not heeded— and yet matters have turned out as I planned!

Despite yourself you were borne across the sea, Prince Askon. Unawares you have brought us the very man we need, if I am any judge.''

Mistirea raised his eyes to the ceiling. ''Perhaps there are other gods, mightier than the spirit of the lake. Perhaps they have guided you, so as to save Peldain.''

''I can't say I ever had the feeling that gods were dictating my actions,'' Octrago commented. ''On the contrary, throughout my adventures I have been afflicted with a feeling of desperate loneliness. The fate of Peldain rested on my shoulders alone, or so I thought.''

He stood and paced the room, then turned to Vorduthe. ''Well, it seems you are going to do some swimming, my lord.''

''Am I?'' Vorduthe replied stonily. ''However noble your motives might seem in your own eyes, I see you in a different light. You have used us for your own ends. You have lied to us, betrayed us, sworn false oaths, sent an army to its death—and not an hour ago I heard you plead that I and my men be murdered. Why should I help you?''

He had no idea what reality might lie behind the extraordinary beliefs Octrago and Mistirea had just propounded, but he was determined to wring what advantage he could from the situation. Mistirea spoke hurriedly.

''Have a care, Prince Askon. Our future may hang on this man's good will. When he communes with the spirit, no one will be by his side.''

''So we have to make a loyal Peldainian of

him?" Octrago said, as if voicing an impossible thought.

"If the soul of Peldain obeys him, he can do good or wreak even worse evil than now threatens."

"What is it you want, my lord Vorduthe?" Octrago asked softly.

"A ship to return my men to the Hundred Islands. Until it is built, they must walk free and unmolested."

"Your men may return, perhaps, but as for you. . . ."

"All lies in the balance," Mistirea interrupted. "Little as you may like it, Prince Askon, communication with the outside world could prove essential to our future survival."

It was clear that Octrago liked the idea not at all. "Well," he said, looking thoughtfully at Vorduthe, "the future is long and much may happen in it. Let him prove himself first."

Chapter Thirteen

The day before Lord Vorduthe was to attempt his first immersion, Troop Leader Kana-Kem had approached him. The seaborne warriors were able to wander at will throughout Lakeside, on promise of good behavior. It was a minimum concession which Vorduthe had extracted in return for his cooperation.

Kana-Kem had been sitting in the shade of an arbor with several comrades, drinking a mildly intoxicating juice that was popular here—though in comparison with the distilled essence of searoot they were used to consuming in shore taverns all around the Hundred Islands, it affected them scarcely at all. He caught up with Vorduthe as he came within sight of the green lake.

"I remind you of your pledge, my lord," he said quietly but firmly. "When do we strike the treacherous snake down?"

"Have patience," Vorduthe told him. "I have a deeper revenge in mind. It may be that I can destroy not only Octrago but this whole rotten kingdom as well. That will be his reward."

He stood now on a mossy bank, Mistirea by his side. The sun shone strongly, halfway between zenith and horizon. Both men were naked. At their feet the edge of the lake rippled slightly in a strong breeze. The dull green water—which Mistirea said was not water at all—was opaque, making the lake look stagnant, though it gave off no smell.

No stream or rivulet fed the lake. Nevertheless Mistirea claimed that it never diminished: it did not evaporate. Rainwater would float on its surface, either to dry off or to be absorbed by the containing banks.

"The time has come," Mistirea said. "Be confident. Let your mind be calm."

Vorduthe made no answer. To his military mind the High Priest's training had seemed strange and incongruous, though he had seen Arelian physicians employ something like it when preparing patients for surgery. By fixing the attention on a steady flame, the mind could sometimes be made oblivious of pain.

In his temple behind the palace, Mistirea had used a similar technique to concentrate Vorduthe's mind, and then had taught him how to turn his consciousness inward. It was like diving into a deep pool, where phantasms of thought drifted. Farther and farther in he went, until thought vanished and there was only a kind of limpid darkness. That, Mistirea said, was where he might meet the soul of Peldain.

Water or not, the substance of the lake felt like water as they waded into it, refreshingly cool to their feet and legs. Then they plunged, and swam for the center.

Mistirea maintained his position with easy motions of his arms. They were floating over the lake's deepest part.

"May the gods who guided you to us aid you now," Mistirea said. "Dive! Dive!"

And Vorduthe dived.

Darkness closed in on him the moment his head slipped below the quiet surface. Not one ray of sunlight penetrated the lake. Down he went, arms streamlined against his sides as though he were diving off the coral atolls that gave Arelia its calm seas.

As he descended he put himself into the semitrance state taught by Mistirea. The darkness grew darker and took on the lightless clarity he had come to know.

Momentarily his attention was distracted. The medium through which he sank became thicker with depth and impeded his motion. Soon he could thrust no deeper and came to a stop, suspended.

Once again he turned his mind inward. Unlike the upper levels, the surrounding fluid was at body temperature. He was losing the sense of his bodily outlines. An impression of beating heart and racing blood filled his consciousness, as though he had become a creature inhabiting his own internal organs. Then that, too, faded.

Mistirea had given him no inkling of what contact would be like, except that it was apt to be unexpected. The spirit of the forest had no solid body and manifested itself according to the mind of the inquirer.

Unexpected it was. Vorduthe almost forgot where he was, almost forgot the need to hold his breath. He was plunged into green light and a mass of green fronds and foliage that stretched away in all directions.

The verdant jungle was not still. It roiled and swelled. Monstrous mutational sports burst from it, quickly to subside and be replaced by others. Fear gripped Vorduthe at first; he thought he was back in the coastal forest. Then he realized that none of this actually touched him. He quieted himself.

In that quiet, he sensed the presence.

Like the jungle itself, it gave the impression of green: the dark, brooding green of the forest's depths or of ancient ferns; the light green of southerly trees; the dazzling luminous green of the glassy gems found on volcanic slopes.

And yet nothing was really visible. The presence was at his shoulder, just outside his range of vision. Now it was here, now it was there. Or he was in a new world and that entire world was alive, in the same way that a person was alive, so that the presence was everywhere and it was nowhere.

But it was real. So real that Vorduthe found himself framing a question.

Where am I?

The answer came in sighs of wind, in the *shush* of waving fronds, in the rustle of foliage and the groan of slender tree limbs.

Where else but here?

Here is only illusion, Vorduthe replied.

Is it? If it is, then everything is illusion.

The voice was becoming strangely firmer. With each succeeding word it seemed to detach itself from leaf and stem, from fern and frond, to become a definite tone: a smooth, confident, green tone. Vorduthe could almost put a face to it, could feel a kind of personality behind it.

Without volition on his part, he plunged deeper into the jungle, which seemed to be of endless depth. Suddenly he was in a little glade, and here a pageant was presented to him. It reminded him of the mythic pageant played out yearly in Arelia, which told how Irkwele, the sky god, made the world. But here the pictures were mind pictures; some of them one could have drawn on sketching bark, some not.

He had already heard something of the story from Mistirea. The lake had poured itself from the sky, where it had once dwelt among the stars. It was a godlike intelligence that had created both the forest and the artifact trees. It had also placed people on the island, to live in harmony with the trees.

For many generations of Peldainians the spirit in the lake had been cooperative, receptive to the trained minds of successive high priests. But now it was growing stronger and intractable.

It was stretching, extending itself. It no longer

wanted to be restrained. Peldain's strange botany was its body, and that body wanted to grow. Peldain as a garden for intelligent animals to live in was an indulgence that no longer mattered. It was to become rank with life, and the mind-jungle surrounding Vorduthe boiled with eagerness.

Vorduthe was glad to see it. This was the revenge he had spoken of to Kana-Kem. He would encourage the spirit in the lake to choke the island.

But what was this . . . he had not counted on the forest being so voracious, so hungry for conquest. It had a greater lust for it than had King Krassos or any of his forebears. Vorduthe saw the forest rage unchecked and invade the sea, mutating all the time.

It would seize the whole world. In time, it would reach the Hundred Islands.

"So now there is a fresh mind to contend with," the green voice said calmly. "Listen, you speak of illusions. You are troubled by dreams. Well, here is a dream."

The viridescent jungle faded. Vorduthe felt his eyes close involuntarily. He was falling asleep.

When he awoke, he felt refreshed. He was lying on a low fleece-covered bed. A pleasant breeze, carrying the tang of the sea, drifted through a nearby open window.

His gaze fell on a ceiling of gaily painted timber, typically Arelian in design. Idly he let his eyes scan the rest of the room, and everything he saw he knew.

He was in his sleeping quarters in his villa, on the headland overlooking Arcaiss.

He leaped from the bed and strode to the window. Far below was the harbor, with trade ships floating at anchor. Partly obscured by the headland were the naval docks, and there he recognized some of the ships that had carried his expedition to Peldain.

The sun had not long risen, and cast dazzling streamers of gold on the flat sea.

For long moments Vorduthe stared at the vivid scene. He did not turn until he heard the sound of the door panel sliding open behind him. What he saw then sent his heart leaping.

The Lady Kirekenawe Vorduthe had stepped into the room. She wore a simple sleeping gown. Her hair fell about her shoulders, and she was smiling.

She moved with all the grace and suppleness he had once known and delighted in.

"I woke feeling different," she said. "So I knew I would find you here."

Vorduthe himself had slept naked, as was his habit. Her eyes were traveling with hungry anticipation over his body, which was stirring.

He reached out. She rushed to him, her body warm and pulsing.

Together, they fell upon the low bed.

The angle of the sunlight falling through the windows had dipped by the time they finished their exertions. They relaxed, luxuriating in each other's aroma.

Suddenly she touched his lips with her fingers. "You must go now. It is time."

"No," he tried to say, but wife and villa rushed from him. He was in darkness, suspended in warm liquid. His lungs ached with the need for air.

No more than two minutes could have passed.

He struck out for the surface. Mistirea was floating there patiently, and he waited while Vorduthe filled his lungs and regained his strength.

Wordlessly they swam to the shore. The two men stood dripping by the lakeside, facing one another.

"You encountered the spirit," Mistirea said. "I can see it in your eyes."

"Yes."

"Can you hold it in bounds?"

"I do not know."

"You must understand how to influence the spirit," Mistirea told him. "Its power is that of a god, but in nature it is elemental, like a young child. You must be the adult that commands that child."

"It no longer is so," Vorduthe said, shaking his head. "The spirit grows. It is maturing like a living creature. It has thrown off its childhood."

Mistirea's eyes blazed with alarm. "Then you must command it as one man commands another! As a king rules a subject! Impose your will!" His voice fell. "I know you have the strength to do this. I am not mistaken in my judgment."

"Perhaps."

"Do not deny it. I am not High Priest of the Lake for nothing. Tomorrow you will dive again."

He handed Vorduthe a thick-napped cloth with which to dry himself. Vorduthe did so and clothed himself. But he refused to accompany Mistirea back to the temple.

Instead he climbed the hill above Lakeside and sat on the fringe of Cog Wood, looking down. He spent a while studying the lake, noting the way it was cupped by the sloping terrain as if it had indeed been dumped from above, supported by an embankment to the west.

If he quieted his mind, after the manner that Mistirea had taught him, he fancied he could almost sense currents of thought running through the network of pale branches over his head. He understood Cog Wood now, since his immersion in the lake's mind-jungle. Within the twisted boughs were what amounted to nerves, and they linked up to form a continuous skein throughout the wood. It was an attempt by the lake, at some time in the past, to create a vegetable version of a brain. Perhaps, he thought, the spirit had intended to transfer itself from the lake to this brain, but the wood had proved unable to sustain consciousness. It was like an arboreal version of some sessile creature, stupid and unmoving, but mentally sensitive to what went on around it.

Apparently even Mistirea did not know the meaning of this past experiment. It, like the sculpted hill-maiden, created at a time when the forest had been much less extensive than it was now, had become lost in the mists of Peldain's history. It never seemed to occur to Peldainians to make a record of events, so that after one generation all was usually forgotten.

Vorduthe's state of enforced calm did not last long. When it broke, his brooding feelings came tumbling through. He still burned for revenge, sickened by Octrago's treachery—even though he could, to a limited extent, understand the motive for the tortured prince's actions.

He had it in his power to exact that revenge. But if he did, Arelia's turn would come. Not immediately—not for a hundred years, perhaps. But it would come, and nothing could stop it.

On the other hand he could exert himself to tame the being in the lake. Vorduthe was used to sizing up a newly met personality, and he sensed that the lake's was not yet stronger than his own. As Mistirea said, it was susceptible. But then, Peldain would be saved, secure within its forest barrier, and Octrago would have triumphed.

Also, Vorduthe could not forget that the lake had powers of persuasion of its own. The problem he contemplated was pushed from his mind by the sweet memory of the interlude the lake had bestowed, which put him in an agony of longing and shame. Longing, because for a brief time it had been as if that fateful accident with the barbsquid had never happened nearly five years ago, as if his wife had remained well and happy. Enthralling dream! Enticing, practically irresistible. . . .

Shame, because even while enjoying the experience he had known that it was not real, and that he enjoyed it alone. In reality his wife lay half a world away, still paralysed, knowing nothing of it.

He despised himself for such solitary indulgence.

A figure in an Arelian kilt was toiling up the slope. As he came nearer Vorduthe saw that it was Troop Leader Kana-Kem. His young face was determined-looking.

He spoke stubbornly. "Forgive me for following you here, my lord. But the men want to know what their orders are to be. Do we strike?"

"Strike?" queried Vorduthe.

"We have not been idle while you have been studying with the Peldainian priest, my lord." Kana-Kem smiled. "We have been working on some of the local girls—they find us pleasing, and have little idea of secrecy. We have found out where the palace armory is. Our weapons are stored there, and much else besides. Now we have but to plan how to get at them."

"I commend you, Troop Leader," Vorduthe said thoughtfully. "What do you suggest we do then?"

"These people are soft, apart from a handful of warriors. We will not be taken by surprise a second time."

"Just the same it would be a risky enterprise, with small chance of success."

"If we do no more than put a sword in Octrago's black heart it will be worth the effort, my lord."

"Yes, we could do that."

Kana-Kem seemed both puzzled and displeased by Vorduthe's diffidence. "You spoke of destroying this kingdom, my lord. If we cannot win it for

King Krassos then that is what we should do. What plan have you?"

"I had intended to arrange for the forest to strangle the whole island," Vorduthe told him bluntly. "But you must keep that to yourself. Do you understand?"

The Troop Leader spent some time in absorbing this news. He nodded, frowning.

"But now," Vorduthe added, "I am not sure. I am not sure . . . I will speak to you again presently."

"The men grow impatient, my lord. You have not spoken to them for days, and they are feeling lost and angry. They will act on their own if you do not give them leadership."

Even this threat of rebellion did not stir Vorduthe. "That is enough," he said sharply. "I will speak to you presently."

Kana-Kem turned and made his way back down the hill. Vorduthe stayed where he was, thinking as he watched the sun glint dully on the green lake below.

Overhead, the gnarled branches creaked in a sudden breeze.

Chapter Fourteen

"I have a hard question to put to you," Mistirea said.

They were in the place referred to as the temple. In reality it was a ceremonial training school where the most suitable of Mistirea's acolytes were taught exercises in psychic sensitivity. The numbers in the temple and its surrounding dwellings were being added to by the armed men from the mountain fastness, whom Mistirea had summoned to Lakeside now that the need to defy King Kerenei was gone. To Vorduthe it was surprising that the High Priest should be permitted his own armed force, even though it was not as large as the king's. Tradition placed a high priority on his safety, evidently.

Shaded from the heat of the day, the room was cooled by large, thick leaves that sprouted from the internal walls and waved constantly. "I have been talking with Prince Askon," Mistirea continued. "He made me realize how little you may wish to help us, beyond the need to save your men from execution.

"It is true that you owe this country nothing. You have suffered much and you have been disappointed in your expectations. In the lake you are alone with the spirit, and it would be easy for you merely to pretend to play the part I have asked of you. After all, only after some time would the behavior of the trees of the forest tell us otherwise.

"If that is your attitude, Lord Vorduthe, then I beseech you to think again. Peldain is a country of thousands of men, women and children, none of whom have done you any harm. Think of them. Think what it would mean if your own country were to be ravaged by this savage forest."

"One Peldainian has done us harm," Vorduthe corrected him, in a flinty voice. "What if I were to demand the blood of Prince Askon as the price of my cooperation?"

"You cannot be serious."

Vorduthe did not answer, only stared stonily.

"The Prince jestingly mentioned the possibility," Mistirea sighed. "Or was it in jest? Yet how could one demand the life of the king's son? Further, King Kerenei is very ill . . . it will not be long before Prince Askon succeeds him. Then we shall have a strange circumstance—the safety of the realm will depend on the king's bitterest enemy."

"Askon Octrago swore himself a vassal of my monarch King Krassos. Let the keeping of his oath be the price of my help."

"In what manner is he to keep it? It can only be a form of words—Peldain remains cut off from the rest of the world, and there is no way your king can rule here."

"I am aware of this." Vorduthe's tone softened slightly. "I have already pondered these matters. You will be relieved to hear that I intend to try my strength against the spirit, if I can. My reasons, however, are my own."

Mistirea appeared satisfied with this response. His judgment of people was intuitive, Vorduthe knew. He depended on feeling to tell him whether a man's word could be taken on trust.

And so it was that later in the day Vorduthe filled his lungs for the second time while floating in the center of the lake. Mistirea placed a hand on the small of his back, urging him down.

Vorduthe dived.

His descent slowed as the liquid thickened, and this time the entity was waiting for him. He entered trance state, and suddenly the darkness was filled with green-gold light.

The voice spoke soothingly. *Come. Come to your beloved wife. Come to Kirekenawe.*

Vorduthe knew that a trap was being opened under him. *These deceptive dreams are a trick,* he replied, speaking in his mind. *You do not take me to my wife. You only present me with my own wishes.*

"You are wrong," the voice told him calmly. "True, when you descend into the lake you descend into your own subconscious mind, the arena where dreams take place. But what you do not know is that this, the undermind, is collective, universal. Everyone shares it. Through it you can contact others, if you know how, and I know how. It is in the undermind that you meet me. There also you met your beloved wife Kirekenawe, the closest to your own soul—*and she met you.*"

"It is not possible. She is half a world away."

"There is no distance in the undermind, just as there is no time. How could a morning pass in the space of one breath? Yet you remember that morning . . . Yes, you dream and she dreams— *the same dream.* And since it is a dream, why should she be paralyzed? Why should you be unhappy? I will create a world for you both where you can find what you lost. . . ."

"It is still only hallucination."

"No, it is as real as anything you have known. Do you think that you dream apart from one another? No, you dream together, your souls meet and you know one another. If you do not believe me, ask her for news of home . . . come, see for yourself . . ."

Vorduthe's resolve to contend with the spirit wavered. That was all the assent the lake needed.

There was a feeling of being drawn through something. A brief period of sleep. Then. . . .

The outrigger boat scudded along on the swelling, shining sea, its triangular sail taut and straining on the slanted spar. Vorduthe leaned on the steering oar, turning the prow of the canoe-like craft while his wife hauled on the sheet, pivoting the sail so as still to catch the wind.

The narrow vessel shot through outcroppings of coral, breasted foamy breaking waves, then beached finally on the sandy shore of the island. Swiftly the Lady Vorduthe reefed the sail and tied the sail-line. They jumped out, splashing through the warm salty water and pulling the outrigger onto the beach together.

The sun sparkled on their sea-bronzed bodies. Vorduthe followed his wife up the beach into the shade of the long-leaved trees whose fruit contained a cool, refreshing drink. He cut down two with his knife, chopping off the stems. They drank their fill, and lay together chewing the sweet yellow pulp.

This little group of tiny islands, completely uninhabited and with an associated atoll, had been a favorite spot of theirs early in their marriage. Many a curved, empty beach had been the scene of their pleasure in one another, while breeze-driven waves crashed softly nearby. But now, after an interlude, Vorduthe recalled the Peldainian lake's advice. He asked his wife how things went in the kingdom.

For the first time a frown crossed her features. "In truth, not well," she said sadly. "Your departure signaled a time of trouble, husband. Must you really hear of it?"

Vorduthe's fist clenched. "Yes!"

"Very well."

She threw down the bell-shaped flower she had been playing with and sat up with her arms around her knees, staring out to sea. "With so many of the seaborne warriors away on the campaign, the

Mandekweans saw an opportunity to revolt. King Krassos sent the remaining warriors to subdue them, not knowing that the Orwanians had secretly joined the rebellion. Near to the Mandekwe reefs the fleet was surprised by Orwanians using fire-canoes. Some ships were burned, some driven onto the reefs, and some managed to put their forces ashore only for them to be destroyed by a larger combined army."

Vorduthe too sat up. "Then it is as Korbar predicted! Except that it was not planned by Octrago. . . ."

"Since then the King has been busy training more warriors and gathering his forces. The rebels have taken some smaller islands and it is known they are assembling a seaborne army of their own. There will be a big sea battle soon. Then, I expect, all will be restored as before. . . ."

Suddenly she jumped up and peered toward the horizon, shading her eyes. "Look! Sails!"

Vorduthe followed her example. He could just see a line of sails which quickly passed out of sight. It was, without doubt, a war fleet.

"We must get back to Arelia quickly," he burst out. "I am needed!"

Her laughter was tinkling, amused, and slightly sorrowful. She turned her eyes to him. "We can do nothing to help, husband. Have you forgotten? We are here, but not here. Elsewhere I lie on my bed, with servants around. As for you, in truth I do not know where you are. Yet somehow I feel that I do not dream all this alone. I feel that you are alive, and with me. Am I right?"

"You are right," he told her. "I am with you. At the same time I am in Peldain, on the other side of the forest."

They sat down again. Haltingly, he told her the story of what had happened since the day his army rolled its engines and wagons into the predatory forest. She listened intently, fascinated, and was silent after he had finished.

"Now I must suffer the frustration of knowing what happens in the Hundred Islands, without being able to come to the King's aid," he added ruefully.

She turned, and clutched his arm. "Let's forget all that," she urged. "Yours is a strange tale, but is not this a better reality than we knew before? Let us enjoy it while we can—together!"

Suddenly Vorduthe realized how thoughtless he had been. His intense joy and delight at being with his wife again, at seeing her restored in her dream body, still could hardly match her own. It was inconceivable that he could rob her of what she had been given. The problems of King Krassos—or of Peldain—dwindled to insignificance.

The sun was lower in the sky, which had darkened marginally to a deeper blue. He sensed that the meeting was over, and took her hand.

Then sleep overtook him.

But he did not wake with aching lungs back in the thickness and the warmth. He was in the green-gold haze, still with no need to breathe.

You see, the lake said, *it is as I told you.*

"What are you?" Vorduthe demanded, framing

the question in his mind. "Is it true that you fell from the stars? That is hard to believe."

"It is true, in a manner of speaking," the lake answered. "I will tell you all, as a gesture of good faith. Once I was a man, not so different from yourself. I came to this world from a world among the stars, in a ship that could fly through the air like a bird. There were no men on Thelessa then. It was I who brought them here.

"Yes, I was a man, but a man with an uncommon ambition. Men are mortal, and my aim was to be immortal like a god. Since it is individuals that die, I needed a body that was not individual, and that would last indefinitely.

"The answer lay in vegetable existence. Vegetable life has a level of consciousness which to us is like deep sleep. This I used as the foundation of my immortality. Upon this sleep I erected the structure of the subconscious mind, the dreaming state, in preparation for receiving my waking consciousness.

"The arrangement is not dissimilar to the human pattern, but the project needed a long, long time, much longer than I had to live. I created the lake as an interim measure. It is not water: it is a biological soup of chemicals upon which I imprinted a replica of my conscious mind, and it is in tune with the great subconsciousness of the forest. This connection already gives me great powers, as you have seen. When the forest is matured I shall take full possession of my new, everlasting, evergrowing body, and the lake will become redundant.

Had the spirit of the lake depended on words only, Vorduthe might have grasped little of what was said. He understood as much as he did with the help of visualizations of hallucinatory vividness, which showed him in glimpsed pictures how this strange long-dead man had descended on Peldain in his flying ship, with a retinue of slaves to help him. He had arranged for future generations of these slaves to be cared for in Peldain's inner garden, in case he still needed human servants. Ironically the cult of the lake had arisen, and unknowingly had retarded culmination of the project. But early on some of the slaves had escaped, had made their way across the sea and settled in the Hundred Islands.

"How could the mind of a man dwell in this lake for thousands of years?" Vorduthe objected. "It would be unendurable."

The spirit laughed gently. "Vegetable existence is not only everlasting, it is also slow. What to you is a thousand years I can experience as one short day, and in that day there has been much to attend to."

"Life as a forest sounds hardly to be desired."

"You lack imagination. Once the time scale is taken into account, there is as much potential in vegetable development as there is in animal. I shall be mobile, I shall sense and think—I shall develop vegetable brains, I shall grow human bodies in pods if I wish. Every tree, every branch and blossom, every new organ and sensation will be at my disposal. Already I experience the sexual excitement of wind-spread fertilization, and had I been able to focus my consciousness in any one place, I would have battled with you in the forest, and destroyed you.

"You would destroy me now, if you could."

"You have guessed that I cannot. I have no power over your will. But there is no need for us to be enemies. I have no interest in the Hundred Islands. I only need Peldain, and not even all of that. Do not oppose me. Leave me in peace, to grow . . . in return, you may come here, and gain your reward . . ."

The glow faded and impending suffocation told Vorduthe that his time was up; the spirit could hold him no longer. He came out of trance state, into blackness, and kicked out for the surface.

The bargain had been struck.

Chapter Fifteen

The tinctures exuded by the medicine trees, the chief aid of Peldainian physicians, no longer were able to sustain the ailing King Kerenei. An air of ceremonial sadness fell over Lakeside at the news of his impending death, mingled with the expectation of his young, vigorous son's accession.

But although Askon Octrago's extraordinary exploit in bringing the foreigners to Peldain had advanced his reputation, the easy-going life of Lakeside was not too much disturbed by these events. Early one morning Vorduthe was visited by Troop Leaders Donatwe Mankas and Wirro Kana-Kem. They walked together through the tree-town. Multicolored blossoms, their perfume ever-present, fell from the arbors and drifted constantly in the air. All around were the parked tree-dwellings, the greater structures that were used as communal meeting places, somewhat of a cross between gardens and taverns. Also there were small workshops where such work as there was to be performed in Peldain was done, and store-houses for food provided by the trees.

No payment was ever demanded for services rendered. The inhabitants were allotted to work as needed, by the authority deriving from the king.

Vorduthe and his companions walked through a crowd of playing children. "We are reaching the point of no return, my lord," Donatwe Mankas complained. "Some of the men are taking wives. Children are on the way. Soon they will feel settled here and will have no stomach to fight. And now Octrago is to be king! Have you given up, my lord? Are we not to strike at all?"

With all the squadron commanders gone, the two remaining troop leaders instinctively spoke up as boldly as if they had held the rank. Indeed, either of these two would make a match for Mendayo Korbar. Kana-Kem glanced at Vorduthe but said nothing. He had never repeated what Vorduthe had told him about his plan to destroy all Peldain, had never even asked what he had eventually decided, but it was plain the warrior thought much.

When he saw these innocent children at play, when he thought of all the blameless families on this island, Vorduthe wondered if he would in fact have the heart to let the entity in the lake proceed, squeezing the habitable area of the island smaller and smaller.

Yet the Eye of Peldain held him to his bargain. Every day he dived into its turbid, tepid depths, and it was as if he dived straight into a secret land below the lake; he no longer encountered the entity at all.

The seeming hours he spent with his wife Kirekenawe meant far more to him than the remaining day here in Lakeside, which paradoxically took on the aspect of a drab dream in comparison. They sailed and swam, they dived in the shallow coral reefs abounding in the Hundred Islands. Sometimes they found themselves somewhere in Arelia, even in Arcaiss—but never again did they meet in their villa: neither of them wanted to come upon the helpless form of Kirekenawe in her quarters. The favorite venue, whether selected by the lake or unconsciously by themselves, was an idyllic little island Vorduthe had never in fact seen, and which he was fairly sure did not really exist: a paradisiacal setting complete with lawnlike meadows, perfumed trees and leaping deer.

Only when pressed did Kirekenawe give him news of the rebellion that King Krassos was fighting to contain. The sea battle, apparently, had been inconclusive. Early on Vorduthe had caught a brief glimpse of damaged and partly burned ships in the harbor. He gathered, however, that there was no immediate danger, and he felt confident that Arelians, as always, would prevail.

Today's would be the sixtieth sojourn, in the dream life, in the distant Hundred Islands.

Vorduthe stopped walking. He looked at the troop leaders one after the other. "You are forgetting that with Octrago's accession to the throne the situation will be changed. He will be in a position to redeem his oath of allegiance. He promised to engineer a way through the forest so as to give regular communication with Arelia, and he should be given a chance to prove his word."

"The project is impossible," Kana-Kem said flatly. "In any case, only a fool would trust him."

These words were close to insubordination. "Enough!" Vorduthe snapped. "I, and I alone, will decide on any action."

Dismissing them, he strode toward the lake.

All Vorduthe's misgivings vanished as the lake's surface closed over his head. A poignant feeling assailed him. Then his consciousness was drawn inward, into sleeplike trance.

He "awoke" on their dream island. He was standing under a water-fruit tree, near a patch of silky tassel-fern. A young leaping-deer with a dappled fawn-colored coat nibbled the moss.

He did not see Kirekenawe at first. But suddenly there she was, gazing at him from the edge of a small grove. Her smile, as he caught sight of her, was wistful, almost pained. She wore nothing but a short kilt of blue-and-purple grass, whose strands moved sensuously as she came toward him.

"Quickly!" she said breathlessly. "Quickly!"

He let her draw him into the silver tassel fern and they sank down in its softness. It was a perfect bed for love-making, and she gripped him with a desperate ardor, more intense than she had ever shown him.

Usually she liked to prolong the pleasure but

now she worked her body with impatient eagerness to satisfy them both as soon as possible. Then, her skin filmed with perspiration, she lay back gasping, gazing at him with soft, sad eyes.

When she had caught her breath she sat up. "Husband, there is little time," she said. "This is our last meeting."

"What are you saying?" he growled in alarm.

Sorrowfully she sighed, shaking her head. "It is not fitting that I should hide the truth from you now, at the very end. I have been less than honest with you—I did not want our newfound happiness to be marred by something we could do nothing to change."

While he stared at her aghast she went on: "The sea battle against the rebels went worse than I told you. It broke Arelia's naval strength. Since then the savages have taken island after island . . . how could I tell you this and make you unhappy? Now the worst has happened. The savages have landed on Arelia . . . King Krassos is dead, Arcaiss is burning and I can smell the smoke . . . the Orwanians have reverted to cannibalism, husband . . ."

Vorduthe recalled with a shock his drugged dream in the forest. "You must have yourself moved at once to a place of safety," he ordered.

"Too late, they are in the house. I hear the servants being murdered. In moments they will enter my room. Good-bye, husband. I die in happiness, knowing what we have enjoyed together!"

"No!"

Vorduthe clutched at his wife. But suddenly she

was not there. He was alone in the tassel bed that was hollowed out by the press of their bodies.

"No!"

This time he cried his protest at the sky. And as if in answer, the world around him trembled and flurried. There was an impression of swift motion. Then he seemed to be looking down on the room where his paralyzed wife lay.

It was impossible to read any emotion in her impassive face. One servant remained with her: a young waiting girl who crouched near her mistress wearing an expression of stark terror. She shrieked as into the room there burst a band of grinning brown-skinned Orwanian primitives, their teeth filed, practically naked except for their weapons.

Laughing, three savages dragged away the kicking, screaming servant girl. The rest turned their attention to Kirekenawe, stripping off the sheet that covered her, playing with her white body. They seemed puzzled at first that she did not move. Then, reaching agreement, they carried her down to the courtyard, where fires had been lit under cooking grids . . . and one Orwanian took a black flint knife to slice off her nose and chew it raw. . . .

At this fulfilment of his earlier premonitory vision Vorduthe's spirit recoiled into the sky among the wheeling birds. The majestic nazarine blue rippled, went dark, and then he seemed to break through a barrier and knew that for him the dream was over.

Images assailed him. He had caught the entity

in the lake unawares and knew that the dream had been no fiction; it really had happened—*was* happening. He saw too how the entity viewed Thelessa: as a dazzling oceanic jewel, a world sapphire, a paradise whose climate varied scarcely at all throughout the year, whose waters remained gentle and pacific. By comparison Vorduthe caught a sense of what other worlds in the heavens were like, tilted somehow with respect to the sun so as to produce extremes of heat and cold all in the same latitude; their seas sloshed about pendulum-like by the near presence of yet other worlds that loomed visibly in their skies.

The entity claimed the whole of Thelessa as its territory, regardless of any bargain struck with Vorduthe. Peldain was to be turned into a single riotous jungle where the vegetable products of a fevered imagination would be given full rein. If any human beings survived, it could only be as hunted animals.

I should have brought you back sooner. I have been inattentive.

The green-gold voice was as smooth and calm as ever, but behind it, keeping pace with its words, was an elemental rage that could not be contained or disguised, a tempest of ever-changing plant growth. The soul in the lake, once a man, had lost its humanity long ago. Vorduthe could dimly understand why. The descent into the subconscious involved a descent into primeval forces. The entity had surrendered itself to the raw wish of primitive life to survive and grow at the expense of anything else.

I see you have resolved to take the part of the High Priest, at last, the voice continued. *You think you can control me.*

In his anger and grief Vorduthe was indeed ready to fight the entity for mastery. But the voice only chuckled.

It is too late, Lord Vorduthe of Arelia. When first you dived into this lake you might have succeeded. But love made you delay, and now I have learned to avoid your will, just as I once learned to avoid Mistirea's. So good-bye, Lord Vorduthe, noble of Arelia.

The voice faded and Vorduthe found himself out of trance state and alone in pitch darkness, warm liquid all around. His lungs had not yet reached the limit of their endurance, but he knew that the entity would never admit him into its presence again.

The lake's stratagem had worked. While Vorduthe was distracted with delight in Kirekenawe it had been familiarizing itself with his psyche, absorbing a part of him so that his mind could not be used as a weapon against it. It was maturing fast. Probably, Vorduthe thought, no one would ever influence it again.

It was time to depart. For the last time he soared, toward daylight and fresh air.

The High Priest's eyes became hollow as Vorduthe, standing dripping on the lake's mossy shore, confessed his failure.

"Yes, I had thought there was something wrong," he said in a ghostly voice. "So it was all for nothing. Peldain will die."

"No," Vorduthe said. "There is still something we can do. If you had not lost the habit of work in the physical world these past generations you would have thought of it yourself."

Mistirea stared uncomprehending when Vorduthe first explained what he meant. When it came home to him that the thing was possible, he was dumbfounded.

"But the Eye of Peldain has always been with us!" he protested.

"Do you still think of it as a god? If so it is a malign god."

"It is a god in a sense, a god that must be appeased . . . yet strange to say, once it was a man." Mistirea nodded, evidently thinking he was telling Vorduthe something new. "Yes, it is so. You know the hill that is shaped like a woman, in the valley beyond the Clear Peaks? Legend has it that the hill was so sculpted on the orders of the lake long ago. Though no longer a man, it became hungry for the shape of a woman. It wished to caress such a woman with the branches of the forest. . . ."

Mistirea came back to the point. "The lake alone can restrain the forest! What would happen if your plan were carried out?"

"But it is not true that the spirit restrains the forest, as such," Vorduthe told him "Rather it is the other way about. The lake is the forest's soul, its driving force. If that force is removed the forest will remain deadly, certainly, but it will have no directing intelligence. It will be unable to evolve; men will be able to drive it back, perhaps even to burn it down. In any case we can prevent it spreading."

Vorduthe began to dry himself. Mistirea stood still, thinking hard.

"It must be done secretly," he said at last. "If the King should hear of it—"

"What of your own acolytes? Could they be trusted?"

"Some, yes . . . others, no."

"My men will carry out the work," Vorduthe promised. "Even if the palace should learn of it, it must still be carried through, and that means fighting. My men alone will not be enough to hold off the King's force, but if even some of your acolyte warriors joined in there might be a chance. Can you get us our weapons? Even more important, we shall need suitable tools."

"Very well, then, we are joined in conspiracy," Mistirea agreed somberly. "If you are wrong, Lord Vorduthe, may the gods you worship help this traitor!"

Chapter Sixteen

It was near dawn of the fourth night when the white-coated acolyte came from Lakeside and touched his brow in the cult's formal sign of respect.

"Our cause is betrayed," he told Vorduthe. "One of us whom Mistirea trusted went to Prince Askon and revealed all. The Prince is on his way here with all the force he could muster."

Vorduthe cursed under his breath. Mistirea had experienced extreme difficulty in judging whom he could confide in. The cult members, long trained in reverence for the lake, found the turn of events confusing.

"And Mistirea?"

"He is gathering your men and those of us we can trust. They too will shortly be on their way here."

"Wait. I will return with you."

Bending his head, Vorduthe stepped into the low, cramped tunnel, shored up by timber props, that ran horizontally into the sloping ground.

Two men came toward him dragging sacks of earth. Even by the light of the lamps he would not have been able to see the other two who were digging at the tunnel's end. They were too far in now, hacking away with tree-grown hardwood tools that were actually meant for replanting trees, but which served their present purpose well enough.

During the daytime the entrance was blocked and concealed. Much easier and quicker would have been to dig straight through the retaining bank, but Vorduthe had elected to start farther down the slope so as to reach a greater depth. By his estimation the tunnel should be about ready to break through.

If he was wrong then the outcome would depend on who won the forthcoming fight. From the cache of weapons stored just inside the entrance he took a sword and strapped on the waist belt and harness. He stopped the two earth-shifters, briefly told them what was happening, and went outside.

In the west the glow of dawn was beginning to challenge the blazing stars. He and the acolyte walked up the slope, skirting the looming bank until eventually they were able to view the dully gleaming, perfectly flat surface of the lake.

They were in time to see a column of men moving among the tree-houses and coming toward the lake. To Vorduthe's military eye they looked like a mob for they came along in a crowd and not in rank and file as Arelian warriors would. Some were garbed in the honey-colored armor of the palace guard, a few in the brown bark cuirasses worn by cult acolytes when in combat order.

Heading them was Askon Octrago, also in honey armor and a coroneted helmet of the same color.

"You would have done better to arm yourself for your errand," Vorduthe observed dryly to the acolyte.

Then, from another direction, Mistirea and Troop Leader Kana-Kem were seen leading a mixed group of seaborne warriors and acolytes round the corner of a large community house. There were about forty Arelians, together with approximately the same number of Peldainians, all armed.

The two groups spotted one another and halted. With feral glances at both Vorduthe and Mistirea, Octrago stepped from among his men. The High Priest, too, moved forward, crossing about half the distance between them.

Octrago's caustic words were crisp on the cool morning air. "Here we have the whole treacherous nest, it seems. Tell me, High Priest, was it for this that I exerted myself? Crossed the ocean? Dared the forest? Well, no matter. You had best not oppose me now. Stand aside while I finish this business once and for all."

"You misunderstand what is happening!" Mistirea's voice was pleading and he addressed not only Octrago but those following him. "We must render the forest harmless, and this is the only way! It should have been done long ago!"

"*What?*" Octrago's face showed that he was genuinely incredulous. "The forest is our protection against the rest of the world! Our ancient hedge—against such as he!" He gestured violently at Vorduthe, glaring. "Your duty is to keep it within bounds, not to strip us of it!"

"It cannot be kept within bounds any longer. We are the lake's prisoners, under sentence of death!" Mistirea puffed out his chest and his voice strengthened. "Listen to me! All I have done, I have done for the sake of Peldain—"

"Your brain has been addled by this lying foreigner," Octrago growled, interrupting. "All this is for the sake of *Arelia!*"

He made a signal to a man behind him. A lance was hurled, catching Mistirea in the chest. He staggered, clutched at himself, then fell to the ground.

With a great shout on both sides, the two forces rushed at one another. The shock of their meeting sounded out a clash of metal and the thudding of lance and sword on timber shields, followed by the grunts, growls and groans of men in mortal combat.

To the Arelians, this was the revenge they had been itching for. They fought like demons, like maddened tentacle-fish, wanting only to hack, stab and kill. The acolytes on both sides had less enthusiasm; they did not like to cross swords with their former intimates and more than one fled the field.

The palace guards, shaken at first by the extent of Arelian ferocity, proved a stiffer foe. Skilled by long practice in the use of shield, sword and lance, they added Arelian as well as Peldainian blood to the stained moss, and the encounter turned into a confused mêlée.

Octrago, however, neatly dodged the fray. He came on straight for Vorduthe, and the unarmed acolyte standing by the commander's side turned and ran, terrified at the sight of the advancing prince, who shouted a challenge.

"*Now* we shall have a reckoning, Lord Vorduthe!"

Having longed to meet Octrago on final terms, Vorduthe was almost glad to see the prince so oblivious of his country's best interests. His sword dropped into his hand and he stood firm to meet the attack.

Neither man carried a shield, but Octrago was quick to take advantage of the fact that he was wearing armor and Vorduthe was not. In the growing daylight his blade shimmered and flickered faster than the eye could follow in feint after feint and, though wise to most tricks of Arelian swordsmanship, Vorduthe found himself forced back by the wild and reckless onslaught.

The rush ended in a straight thrust to the heart which Vorduthe barely deflected in time and Octrago's point gouged his shoulder. With renewed rage he went on the attack. They came to close quarters. For some moments the two men swayed together, then they sprang apart, weighing one another up warily.

"*The lake! Look at the lake! The lake!*"

All fighting stopped as, in silence, those on both sides obeyed the hysterical shout that had come from among them. The rim of the sun was visible on the western horizon now. By its light the surface of the lake shimmered, rippled, swirled.

Taking care to keep Octrago visible out of the corner of his eye, Vorduthe half-turned to look behind him. A flood of green liquid was pouring down the sloping terrain from the tunnel that had been dug in it. The diggers, having been carried by the onrush, were picking themselves up, staggering and sloshing to safety.

The same voice as before let out a despairing wail.

"They are draining the lake!"

"You have murdered the soul of Peldain!"

This last came from Octrago. Face contorted, he came at Vorduthe with such berserk fury that the Arelian commander was forced into the lake. Octrago followed him and seemed to have abandoned all thought for his own life. Soon the two were up to their waists and slashed wildly at one another, floundering.

Vorduthe felt an undertow tug at his legs. Then, as he shifted his footing, the bottom fell away beneath him and he toppled.

A strong current caught him. He went under, dragged down and toward the far side of the lake where the tunnel had broken through. His sword snagged on the bottom and was torn from his grasp, then something seized his leg and began clawing its way toward his throat.

It was Octrago; the Peldainian prince had lost his sword too but now was intent on killing him with his bare hands. In utter darkness, swept along by the increasingly swift current, they struggled.

At last Vorduthe felt the other grow weaker. He pushed him away and sought to strike for the surface, but the current was now far too strong. Down he went, and there, in the surging dark, he became aware of an emotion.

It seemed to be all around him in the moving liquid: stark fear, disbelief, a terrible desire not to succumb to death.

The mind in the lake had begun its disintegration. Undisturbed for thousands of years, its substance was moving, whirlpooling, draining away. Vorduthe's consciousness went blank; involuntarily he found himself entering trance state, and before him there seemed to hover a gigantic face.

Momentarily he saw it clearly: vaguely of Peldainian cast, chalk-white, with straw-colored hair and glaring blue eyes. It was this face that emitted the emotion Vorduthe had been feeling. The eyes were desperate, savage in their protestation of what was happening. The lips moved, mouthing an accusation he could not hear.

For the huge visage was distorting. It was a face drawn on water, and the water was moving, streaming, pouring and whirling toward some outlet to one side.

Vorduthe came to normal awareness. He had not filled his lungs properly when he went under but did not have the strength to regain the surface. He realized that his best chance of survival would be to go with the stream and hope to be carried through the tunnel. He began to swim, trying to reach the center of the maelstrom whose outlet was at the far bottom of the lake.

His lungs strained for air. He bumped into something, was sucked into a thick confusion of mud and detritus. Vaguely he was aware of being carried along at speed, then his senses gave out.

When he came to, Donatwe Mankas and Wirro Kana-Kem were dragging him clear of a widening swamp of moss and green fluid. He forced himself to his feet, waved them away and looked out over the scene, breathing deeply.

The green lake was still pouring through the tunnel mouth. Hours would pass, perhaps, before it all drained away. Kana-Kem indicated a limp figure lying some distance from the tunnel, gradually being pushed down the slope by the flow. "That is Askon Octrago, my lord. Washed out like a dead fish. He could not dive like an Arelian!"

Vorduthe looked at the pathetic form with mixed feelings. "In some ways he was noble of soul," he admitted. "He achieved remarkable things, despite his methods . . . such determination has to be admired."

"His father, King Kerenei, died last night," Mankas added. "He was a king himself, yet he came and fought you personally. That, too, was brave."

Vorduthe sighed. "What of the rest of it?"

"We have won the day already, my lord. The heart went out of the Peldainians when the lake started to move, and even more so when their

King Askon failed to surface! Most are dead, a few are taken prisoner."

"Then it is all ours," Vorduthe said. He stared into the rising sun. "This land was falsely promised to our monarch. We shall take the liar at his word. I claim Peldain in the name of King Krassos, his heirs or successors."

"We still are few—even fewer, now. It is a big place."

"Who is there to oppose us? The common inhabitants have no spirit of resistance, and besides their god has been destroyed."

How could he explain what he knew, and how he knew it? That King Krassos was dead, the Hundred Islands torn apart by insurrection, Arcaiss sacked. Peldain would have to be put to work, a path cleared through the forest, ships built, an army of warriors trained. It was their task now to return to the Hundred Islands and restore Arelian greatness.

How long would it take? No matter. They would do it.

"First we secure this country," he said. "Then back to the Hundred Islands. Arelia needs us."

The strengthening sun was beginning to hurt his eyes, but he did not remove his gaze. He was glad of the excuse for tears.

For his thoughts were in Arelia. He was thinking of the villa on the headland. And only now could he dwell on his grief.